John Humphreys Davies

Some Welsh Legends and Poems

Second Edition

John Humphreys Davies

Some Welsh Legends and Poems
Second Edition

ISBN/EAN: 9783744765145

Printed in Europe, USA, Canada, Australia, Japan

Cover: Foto ©Andreas Hilbeck / pixelio.de

More available books at **www.hansebooks.com**

SOME WELSH LEGENDS

AND OTHER

POEMS.

BY

JOHN H. DAVIES, M.A.

SECOND EDITION.

Sudbury:

PRINTED AND PUBLISHED BY HENRY C. PRATT.

1893.

PREFACE.

A few words by way of Preface. In the first place I inscribe this book to my friends. Secondly, I wish to thank Messrs. Cassell & Co. for the kind permission, so readily accorded me, to reprint from *The Quiver* and *Cassell's Magazine* the poems "The Dear Old Face," "A Cloud with a Silver Lining," and "A Perfect Day in June," of which they hold the copyright. Thirdly, I acknowledge most gratefully the service rendered me by Mr. Hamilton Robinson, Mus. Bac., F.C.O., Organist and Director of the Choir of St. Stephen's, South Kensington, in revising the harmonies of the tune "Vox Stellarum."

J. H. D.

New Year's Eve, 1892.

INDEX.

PART I.

WELSH LEGENDS.

SHUI RHYS.

Adown the lane at day's decline
A dark-haired maiden blithely goes,
Her eyes with mirth and mischief shine,
Her cheeks more ruddy than the rose,
And tripping, skipping by her side
Queer little creatures move and glide;
And in her ear sounds music sweet,
That bids her heart with rapture beat.

The kine are lowing in the mead,
And wait, impatient, Shuï's call;
For brimming teats relief they need,
And comfort in the cosy stall.

But Shuï loiters, heeding not,
Her errand, home, and all forgot ;
So strange the tales the fairies tell,
Who guide her to the Goblin's Well.

The kine come lowing up the lane,
Untended to the farmyard gate,
Dies in the west the day again,
And "Shuï, Shuï, why so late?"
In shrilling accents mami cries,
But no sweet voice to-night replies :
Far, far away, by fairies led,
The foolish little maid is sped.

Her father sought her high and low,
Her mother sighed and moaned and wept,
Through the wild wood they searching go,
And three long nights has neither slept.
No trace, no sign appeared at all,
No voice made answer to their call ;
Save that there came, the gossips tell,
Weird laughter from the Goblin's Well.

THE BELL BENEATH THE SEA.

On Rosson Rock* at day's decline,
　A lonely stranger stands
(A wanderer he for many days
　In unfamiliar lands)
Listing a sound, in boyhood's prime
　Oft waited for with glee,
As slowly swung and, muffled, rung
　The bell beneath the sea.

His sad, dark eyes surveyed a scene
　Unchanged in all the years—
The barren heights, the beetling crags,
　Allt-felen-fawr† uprears ;
And ever, with the tides that there
　So wild and restless be,
Chimed from Gafaeliog's‡ treacherous reef
　The bell beneath the sea.

---

* Rosson Rock, near St. David's, Pembrokeshire, and overlooking Ramsey Sound.

† The highest precipice of Ramsey Island.

‡ A dangerous rock at the northern entrance of the sound.

"Afar, all rosy in the light
  Of evening, Whitesand Bay
Glows glorious, and the bluff old Head
  Smiles farewell on the day.
Alas! If kind to these, grey Time
  Deals otherwise with me!
No more, a boy, I hear with joy
  The bell beneath the sea.

None hears it now, but he whose heart
  Clings fondly to the past;
For him its mournful music swells
  Unearthly on the blast,
To tell of joys long lost, to warn
  Of sorrows yet to be—
Seek ye this spot who doubt it not,
  The bell beneath the sea.

How came it there? Long years have flown
  Since high in yonder tower,
Its deep-toned voice to matins called
  The monks of Bishop Gower.

Age after age—monk—prelate—priest,
  Away like shadows flee!
Still for their souls a requiem tolls
  The bell beneath the sea.

Erst, with its silvery brethren seven,
  Down Alan's winding dale
The jocund chimes it sent at times
  Sonorous on the gale;
But stern, Gafaeliog's jaggèd rocks
  To greedy Saxons be—
Now fathoms deep our mermen keep
  The bell beneath the sea.

Five hundred years! Five hundred more!
  And what will then remain ·
Of creeds which now we scarce believe,
  Half-pagan grown again?
All that is mortal-made must pass
  Into obscurity;
But cease what may, rings on for aye
  The bell beneath the sea.

At morn, at eve, at midnight's hour,
  All seasons, foul or fair,
Through ocean's aisles its notes resound,
  And call the dead to prayer.
And ever, till the crack of doom,
  '*Laus tibi, Domine!*'
At ebb and flow will murmur low
  The bell beneath the sea."

So mused the stranger as he stood
  On Rosson's rugged brow,
Recalling legends of the past
  The faithless sneer at now,
And heard the voice of by-gone years
  Put forth its solemn plea,
Where slowly swung and, muffled, rung
  The bell beneath the sea.

THE LADY OF LLYN-Y-VAN

I.

A voice from the slope of the mountain,
  A voice from the hazel brake,
Calling, calling, calling
  The cattle out of the lake.

Ah, maid with locks so golden
  And cheeks of rosy hue,
Why hast thou pierced the shepherd's heart
  With flashing eyes of blue,
Tripping, tripping, tripping
  Down the mountain side,
Thro' the hazel brake to the brink of the lake,
  Where the fairy cattle hide?

" Stay, maiden, gentle maiden,
  One moment, I implore,
For never on those hills was seen
  A face so sweet before!"

" I may not pause, young shepherd,
    Stern duty's path I take,
Calling, calling, calling
    The cattle out of the lake."

" Yet maiden, gentle maiden,
    Thou wilt not be unkind !
Nay, doom me not for ever
    To misery of mind ! "

"Ah shepherd, silly shepherd,
    What would'st thou have with me ?
A child of the Mystic People,
    I may not talk with thee."

" Ah, say not so, fair maiden,
    Though humble be my lot,
Yet would'st thou deign to share it,
    A palace were my cot."

"Ah, shepherd, silly shepherd,
    If I gave heed to thee,
What promise and what pledges
    Would'st thou make good to me ?"

" Ill give thee frankly, freely,
　　Of all that is my store ;
I'll cherish thee for ever,
　　And love thee more and more."

" Ah ! shepherd, oaths are easy
　　For faithless swains to vow—
Perchance thou wilt prove cruel
　　Who art so gentle now."

" Doubt that the grass grows green, love,
　　Doubt that the sun shines fair,
But deem not thou thy faithful swain
　　Would so himself forswear."

"Ah ! shepherd, silly shepherd,
　　I plight my troth to thee,
Nor shalt thou say, ' The Fairies' child
　　Came portionless to me.'

" Rich dower of kine I'll bring thee,
　　Black cattle from the lake ;
And for thy love I'll love thee,
　　Be thine for thy sweet sake.

"But, oh, remember duly,
   Or it may vex thy heart,
Should aught of iron touch me,
   That instant I depart!"

A voice from the slope of the mountain,
   A voice from the hazel brake,
Calling, calling, calling,
   The cattle out of the lake.

There's a great black bull in the meadow
   None saw there heretofore;
Strange oxen over the upland
   Plod on the plough before.

They came to her up the valley,
   They followed her up the steep,
Forth from the midst of the waters,
   Where the Van lies dark and deep.

Oh, joy for the silly shepherd!
   Oh, joy for the life of bliss,
Which surely, surely waits him,
   Spouse of a bride like this!

Oh, joy for the light condition
    So easy to fulfil,
When love is lord of the hearts of both,
    And lord shall be there still !
A voice from the slope of the mountain,
    A voice from the hazel brake,
Calling, calling, calling
    The cattle out of the lake.

From shore to shore the waters foam,
As the fairy brings her dowry home.

II.

A voice from the slope of the mountain,
    A voice from the hazel brake,
Calling, calling, calling
    The cattle back to the lake,
Ah, maid with locks dishevelled,
    And cheeks of pallid hue,
Why dost thou quit thy loved one's cot
    Tears in thine eyes of blue ;

Pacing slowly, slowly
　　Down the mountain side,
Seeming to shrink from the dark lake's brink
　　Where the fairy cattle hide?

　"Ah, lady, cruel lady,
　　　What have I done to thee?
　Is this thy plighted promise?
　　Is this thy faith to me?"

　"Ah, shepherd, foolish shepherd,
　　The iron grazed mine arm;
　Now broken is our marriage bond
　　And shattered is the charm!"

　"Ah, lady, cruel lady,
　　Thou dost not well to fly
　From one so true and tender—
　　Come back, or I shall die!"

　"Ah, shepherd, foolish shepherd,
　　Thou can'st not alter fate;
　Thou should'st have aimed with better aim
　　But now it is too late."

A voice from the slope of the mountain,
A voice from the hazel brake,
Calling, calling, calling
The cattle back to the lake.

The great black bull in the meadow
Is seen no more there now,
No more her stalwart oxen
Plod on before the plough.

Bellowing down the valley,
Thundering down the steep,
They plunged with her 'neath the waters,
Where the Van lies dark and deep.

Alas for the silly shepherd !
Alas for the broken spell !
Alas for the years of wedded bliss
That passed away so well !

Alas for the iron bridle,
Hurled at the steed that fled !
Alas for the luckless hand that threw
And struck the wife instead !

No voice from the slope of the mountain
  No voice from the hazel brake,
Calling, calling, calling
  The cattle out of the lake !

The waters are smooth from shore to shore,
And kine and fairy return no more !

EINION LAS

I.

Warm was the wind of summer,
　　Fair lay the vale below,
As he climbed the steep of the green hill-side
　　Three hundred years ago ;
And oh ! for the throstle singing
　　High on the birchen tree,
And oh ! for the music ringing
　　Over the daisied lea !
At the cromlech's foot he sat him down
　　To listen to that bird—
Never a song so sweet before
　　Had ear of mortal heard,
Singing, tenderly singing,
　　In strains so blithe and bright,
Of the world that lies beyond this world
　　In everlasting light.
No more the gray old mountains,
　　From childhood loved and known,

No more the tranquil valley,
　Were to his vision shown ;
All scenes familiar vanished,
　And kith and kindred fled,
He saw around him marvels
　In rich abundance spread.
And, wandering in a garden
　Of rapture, love, and joy,
His heart was light within him,
　No more a shepherd boy.
Here flowers of rarest beauty
　Would coyly bar his way,
There tinkling fountains spouted
　A dewy-diamond spray ;
And stately palms above him
　A pleasant murmur made,
And groves of bay and myrtle
　Invited to their shade.
In palace-halls of splendour
　Did golden dishes shine,
And flashed from crystal goblets
　The ruby rays of wine,
And circling ever round him,

Or tripping at his side,
The sweetest forms and faces
  He constantly descried.
And oh! for the ring they danced in,
  So nimbly and so fleet,
And oh! for the eyes that glanced, in
  Allurement soft and sweet!
And oh! for the throstle singing
  High on the birchen tree,
And oh! for the music ringing
  Over the daisied lea!

II.

Keen was the wind of winter,
  Dark was the vale below,
As down from the steep came Einion Las
  Two hundred years ago.
And oh! for the raven croaking
  High on the withered tree,
And oh! for the chill mist soaking
  Into the dreary lea!
At his own house door he paused and drew

B

A hand across his brow ;
"It was summer," he said, "when I went hence,
  And is it winter now ?
Moaning, dismally moaning
  The wind has wrought a change !
O, Einion Las, what means it all ?—
  Why has the world grown strange ? "
To the door an old man tottered,
  Who saw an old man there,
Whose face was seamed and wrinkled,
  And sparse his snow-white hair.
" And who art thou ? " cried Einion,
  In accents sharp and shrill,
' Where is my father ? Tell me ;
  And is my mother ill ? "
" I know thee not," said the other ;
  " What dost thou at my door ?
Long years I have lived at Frennifach,
  But ne'er saw thee before."
" Thy door ! " he answers hotly,
  " This is my father's home !
I am Einion Las, the shepherd boy,
  Back from the mountain come !

And there, as I sat by the cromlech,
　Under the birchen tree,
The throstle sang this morning
　The sweetest song to me."
"'This morning,' saidst thou?—'Einion Las'?—
　What news I hear to-day!—
Why, man, 'tis now a hundred years
　That Einion went away!
Long since my father's father
　Who was thy father, died;
But thou art welcome, uncle,
　I pray thee step inside!"
A hand he stretched in pity.—
　It grasped the formless air,
For, crumbling into dust, behold,
　No Einion Las was there!
And oh! for the raven croaking
　High on the withered tree!
And oh! for the chill mist soaking
　Into the dreary lea!

PART II.

General Poems.

PART II.

GENERAL POEMS.

—

BE NOT UNKIND.

Be not unkind!
So little now remains to me
Of youth and hope, I pray thee be
Gentle and tender to me, mindful how
This farewell we are taking now
May prove the last;
Think of the bright hours past,
Nor marvel if with clouded face I sigh
When we shake hands, sweetheart, and say

"Good bye."

Be not unkind !
So little now remains to me
Of sweet in life, I pray thee be
Somewhat less petulant than is thine use ;
For pity's sake do not refuse
One parting kiss !
From thy full store of bliss
'Twere but a trifle to let pass away,
And yet—to me—wealth more than I could say.

Be not unkind !
So little now remains to me
Of time and tide, I pray thee be
Not cold and cruel, only for one hour !
Soon, soon enough, dark skies will lower,
Life's ocean frown,
And my poor bark go down
When the mad storm sweeps by, and I am sped
To far dim depths of the unloving dead !

THE LANDING-PLACE AT THE MERE.

One day comes back to my memory, sweet,
  In the summer of the year,
I had rowed you over the broad expanse
  Of the rippling sunlit Mere.
Wild rose, forget-me-nots, your hands
  Round a lily-star did twine—
Your thoughts were full of the tender task,
  And you were the flower in mine!

A rapture I felt men feel but once
  In life, and nevermore,
As our fingers met for a moment's space
  When the boat drew in to shore.
Oh! the bright and beautiful landing-place,
  Where the sun streamed through the trees :
I see you now, as I saw you then,
  On the bank, in graceful ease,

Lingering, twisting that wild-flower wreath
  Round a spray of the old thorn tree ;
Ah, why did your eyes meet mine, dear maid,
  As if you cared for me?
I dreamt a dream, a wild, sweet dream,
  A day-dream—false, untrue ;
There was nought in the world but lovelier seemed
  For the love I bore to you !

And my life was full of a light divine,
  And my heart with hope beat high,
And the path I trod lay clear and fair
  Beneath a cloudless sky.
Darling, darling, how changed the scene
  Since the day that I recall ;
There is nought in the world, I think, the same—
  Aged, altered, one and all !

Parted, estranged, we meet no more,
  And I but vainly yearn,
For the joy and the hope, and the light divine,
  That never will return !

Oh! dreary, desolate, landing-place,
  On the cold and sunless Mere;
Through the withering fronds of the old thorn tree
  The wind wails all the year!

No dog-rose trails its clustering buds
  Down to the water's edge,
Nor lily, nor blue forget-me-not,
  Shows from the seething sedge.
Only the moor-hen fitful sends
  Her melancholy cry;
And chill and lone is the path I take
  Beneath a frowning sky.

A FAREWELL.

(Lines written to be set to music.)

Farewell, young Love ! A long farewell !
  I leave thee with an aching heart ;
Go, teach some other throb and swell,
    But we must part.

Farewell, young Love ! Thy radiant smile
  May flood with light my path no more :
All happiness I knew awhile—
    'Tis past and o'er !

Ay me ! Thou wast so kind, so sweet,
  I would it had been all a dream !
Life's shadows but the darker meet
    For this brief gleam.

Farewell, farewell ! Our diverse ways
  Through the lone world we take in pain :
God knows if " after many days "
    To meet again !

Much teen my future bodes me yet,
  But golden still and gay be thine !
Live, and be happy, and forget—
    Be memory mine !

THE OLD YEAR.

I dreamt last night I was standing
  On the shore of an awful sea,
That stretched in its terrible splendour
  Far out and away from me ;
And a little boat lay rocking
  At anchor thereon hard by,
And the sun was set, and the winter night
  Scowled from the eastern sky.

Down to the strand with tottering steps,
  Beneath a burden vast,
Sighing and muttering to himself,
  Methought, an old man passed.
In haste o'er the sand and the shingle
  Toward the boat he made,
Eager as one whose going
  Has been too long delayed.

" Whither away, when the sun is set,
  Mariner, answer me,
Art bound to-night, in a craft so frail,
  Across that awful sea ?

Thy hands are feeble, thy back is bent,
   Thou art weary and worn and old,
Go back to the ingle, foolish man,
   And warm thee from the cold ! "

" I am the Year departing,
   I dare not pause or stay ;
I must launch me on yonder ocean.
   And voyage far away.
God knows I am bowed and feeble,
   And weary and worn and old,
But here for me may no ingle be
   To warm me from the cold ! "

" Say, what is the heavy burden
   Thou bearest with such pains ?
Carriest thou hence to another world
   A twelvemonth's golden gains,
Rich profits which thou, by prudence
   And skill in the marts of earth,
Hast drawn from the wares thou hast trafficked in,
   And bales of costly worth ? "

" Not so," he answered sadly,
　Shaking his grizzled head,
And oh, for the groans he uttered,
　And oh, for the tears he shed !
" I have laboured on earth for nothing,
　I have spent my toil for naught,
No golden gains have I gained at all
　From the costly bales I brought !

And the burden that weighs upon me
　And bows me down so low,
Is the burden of hours and minutes
　That reckless men let go—
The burden of fair occasions
　By millions never seized,
When wrongs were to be righted,
　And aching bosoms eased ;

The burden of gentle speeches
　Lips should have spoken here,
That together with kindlier actions
　Had made some lives less drear

The burden of all the gladness
That in this world might be,
Had men but thought of the Giver more,
Who took God's gifts from me !"

" Alas ! in that heavy burden
What sins thou hast of mine !
Oh. mariner, give them back to me,
For bitterly I repine,
Thinking of fair occasions
And days and moments sped,
And the work for God I might have done
If I their rede had read !"

" Too late ! too late !" was the solemn voice
That answered from the shore,
" The Past is past, but the years to come,
See that thou waste no more !
And now—for I hear the summons
That brooks no fresh delay—
A long farewell and a sad farewell
To earth and thee I say !"

Weeping, bitterly weeping,
   Into the boat he stept,
And rowed out into the darkness
   That over the waters swept.
Bearing his burden with him,
   That burden strange and vast,
And weeping, bitterly weeping,
   Beyond my vision passed.

Sadly, methought, I turned me
   From the shore of that awful sea,
And I knew that its terrible splendour
   Was that of Eternity ;
And my heart was troubled within me
   And heavy with many fears,
And lo !—it was New Year's morning,
   And I awoke in tears !

c

HARVEST HOME.

Adown the dusty lanes all day,
  The lumbering wagons rolled,
And stript and bare, the captive fields
  Delivered up their gold.

High in the haggard rose the stacks,
  All working with a will,
And now the horkey load alone
  Remains ungathered still.

The great round sun, as red as blood,
  Went down an hour ago,
And all the cloudland of the west,
  Reflects his afterglow.

Up from the river like a ghost
  The mist begins to rise,
And the brown owl from his old oak
  Stares with wide-open eyes.

From distant breck, the partridge now
  Dares call his scattered brood,
And, rustling thro' a gap, the hare
  Makes t'wards the ley for food.

While yonder, on the Eastern ridge
  That the horizon bars,
Behold a scintillating spark—
  The ruddy planet Mars.

With shouts and cheers, gay laugh of girls,
  With merriment and glee,
The horkey load comes home at last
  Across the dewy lea.

Hurrah! Hurrah! The foaming cans,
  Go round—are emptied quite!—
"God bless the master and the man!"
  "God bless us all!—Good night!"

ON SEEING A PHOTOGRAPH OF MYSELF, AGED NINE.

O little lad, light-hearted elf,
   With laughing eyes and open brow,
Art thou indeed my former self?
   Ah, not the self that I am now!

So long ago! 'Tis like a dream
   Here to recall those far-off days:
Awhile the shadowy visions gleam,
   And mock, confused, my eager gaze.

One moment, 'tis the transient sheen
   Of summer skies and fields and flowers;
The next, how wildly changed the scene,
   For darkness glooms and winter lowers!

Here—but a glimpse!—a rustic lane,
   Where ev'ry gale soft fragrance breathes,
And round one gnarled old thorn again,
   The lush wood-bine its tendril wreathes.

There, whilst afar the murmuring brook
  Reflects the dewy moon of May,
A brown bird in the hazel-nook—
  Hark! how he sings his soul away!

Next, with a glow that seems to blind,
  July's warm sun, one cloudless morn,
And swaying in the southern wind
  The poppies and the golden corn!

Then, in a trice, the chestnut falls,
  Ripe from the autumn-burnished tree,
And to his mate the partridge calls
  At sundown o'er the stubbled lea.

O little lad, the by-gone years
  Thus rise before me, pause, and pass,
And in them all your face appears
  As clear as on this sun-limned glass.

I see you in the house, where oft
  A crazy step-dam's wrath ran wild
(Gentle at times to you, and soft),
  A dreamer even when a child!

Now, by the fireside o'er a book—
   A pictured Shakspeare, is it not?—
You bend and pore with raptured look,
   The wintry world outside forgot.

Now, in your play-ground out of doors,
   Building sand-forts you vex your brains,
Or, slowly moving on all fours,
   Push on your wooden railway trains,

Now, by the plodding ploughman's side
   You air your lore with boyish glee;
Now, condescend to sink your pride,
   His pupil for a space to be.

How many times you try and fail!
   (So Giles the sum upon your slate!)
But perseverance must prevail—
   At last you draw a furrow straight!

(Ah me! Ah me! my little lad,
   One, sick of manhood's aimless strife
Deems it were better if he had
   Drawn straight the furrow of his life!)

Now, where the sluggish river creeps
   Past rustling reeds and osier-car,
You wade adown its pebbly deeps,
   And happy as a king you are !

Now, where the ruined abbey flings
   Its shadow o'er the grassy plain,
I hear a voice—'tis yours—that sings
   In careless mood a jocund strain.

Now, in the croft, tough " cocks-and-hens "
   In either hand you portion well—
Your mimic soldiers !—tens by tens—
   What myriads in those battles fell !

The cruel war went raging on
   'Twixt Grant and Lee, and did not lag !
There, victory always smiled upon
   The brave Virginian leader's flag !

Now, grave, you climb the westward hill
   With dewy eve before the stars :
What scenes of beauty rise at will
   Beyond *your* sunset's crimson bars !

Unutterable ecstasies
   Flood, as you look, your soul with joy ;
Seems your lost mother from the skies
   To lean and bless her orphan boy !

Now, by the water-mill at night,
   Sudden you pause and skyward gaze,
Awe-struck beneath a wondrous sight—
   The mighty comet's lurid blaze !

Ah ! child, you were not far from God,
   I think, in those far distant years,
You had not felt His chastening rod,
   Nor shed despair's remorseful tears !

And well for you, if you, the man,
   Had kept your faith as free from stains,
As when a careless boy you ran
   About those distant woods and lanes !

   *   *   *   *   *   *   *   *

So, one by one, past scenes arise,
   Me gazing on myself the child,
Light-hearted elf, with laughing eyes,
   And soul by sin not yet defiled.

And aye returns one vision still,
  Now lost, now seen on mem'ry's wave,
A little church upon a hill,
  And near its porch a little grave.

Scant hope for me the future keeps :
  Dimmed are mine eyes and lined my brow;
But in that grave my brother sleeps,
  I would that I were with him now !

AT SUNDOWN BY THE SEA.

Day is passing ; cold and cheerless night is creeping
    o'er the sky ;
All the sounds of mirth and music quickly into
    silence die ;
Vanished is the golden sunshine ; only, where the
    great orb set,
Some refulgence of his glory lingers on th' horizon yet.

How the waters gleam and glitter yonder where the
    deep sea rolls !
What a path of splendour opens, trodden by un-
    numbered souls,
Leading onward, onward ever to the pearly gates afar,
To the land of rest unending, where the things eternal
    are !

Ah, that home of calm and comfort, sweetest haven
    of delight,
How we long at last to reach it ere the closing-in
    of night !

Tossed with waves and tempest - driven, battered,
  smitten, sore distressed,
Yet to hope persistent clinging and the full reward
  of rest.

When I reach my day's declining and the sundown
  of my life,
And my weary eyes are turning from earth's scenes
  of care and strife,
Rise, O Vision, then to bless me, shine, True Light,
  at close of day
Like an afterglow of even over waters far away.

HIS DEAD.

I.—ROME, B.C. 95.

Why gaze you on that silent couch ?
   What spell detains you there ?
There is no presence in the room
   Save that of full despair ;
No recognition in the eyes
   Whose steadfast glance you dread ;
Nor love nor friendship in the smile
   On those pale features spread !

" She sleeps," say you ?—Deluded one,
   Say is that sleep the same
As when, she murmuring in her dreams,
   You stooped to catch your name ?
Mark how her lips are curled and set,
   Almost, methinks, a sneer,
Scorning what doom might lie *beyond*,
   And weary of all *here !*

Come nearer ; print th' impassioned kiss
   Upon her clay-cold brow ;
Call her by each endearing word—
   She will not answer now !
Fondle those locks, wherein of old
   The glorious sunshine strayed ;
A shadow over all has crept,
   And darkens ev'ry braid !

Nor wine, nor love, nor dulcet airs
   Of cithern or of flute
Can wake again the voice you loved,
   Inexorably mute !
" Lydia, farewell, a long farewell,
   A last farewell ! " you cry ;
The pitiless gods regard you not,
   Still smiles the changeless sky.

II.—ROME, A.D. 95.

Her hands are crossed upon her breast
   And on her tranquil face
There falls a glorious light, as if
   From some celestial place

God suddenly had shewn Himself,
  And beckoned her away,
The poor slave-girl, to lands of love
  And everlasting day !

Yes, Claudia "sleeps," but not the dull,
  Dark sleep of nevermore
That wakes, at best, in cheerless gloom
  On sad Cocytus' shore !
Light, to the world revealed at last,
  And victor o'er the grave,
Has brought to man undying hopes,
  To cheer, console, and save !

And kneeling by his dear one's side
  In humble, heartfelt prayer,
Syrus commits her soul to Christ,
  And not to long despair ;
His faith, for all the darkness here,
  Has grasped the things above ;
He knows that her Redeemer lives ;
  He feels that God is love.

With sober joy almost he sees
   The golden gates unbar,
And shining ones of Heaven come forth
   Upon each brow a star,
With " Welcome, welcome ! " to the saved,
   Called home to perfect rest ;
Then rising from his knees, content,
   Has peace within his breast.

HER NEW YEAR'S EVE.

The cold is bitter in the street
Like fire it burns my shoeless feet,
Unpitying as the looks I meet.

Outside the house—his house—I stand,
Once happiest maiden in the land,
Now the loathed wretch of all men banned!

I see him standing in the light,
By the warm ingle-side so bright,
And not one thought for me to-night!

Only a year ago, and now
He breathes in other ears the vow
That flushed with joy my cheeks and brow!

In there, where all looks home and gay,
The child he calls his "love" to-day;
Out here, the love he cast away!

What if I tapped the window-pane,
And looking out, he saw again
The haggard face that once was Jane?

Ha! Ha! He would not recognise,
In sunken cheek and famished eyes,
The features he was wont to prize!

So! I have seen my last of him!
The snow falls thick, the lamps burn dim,
I seek the river cold and grim.

THE GOLDEN CITY OF LOVE AND REST.

(Lines suggested by seeing the planets Venus, Mercury, Mars, and the
Moon together in the western heavens, February 28th, 1887.)

O born of the foam of the sheeny sea
   In the sunlit bay of the land Elysian,
Goddess, again thy star for me
   Unseals in heaven the dazzling vision,
Flashing afar, o'er the waters west
From the golden City of Love and Rest.

Zoned with diamonds, sandall'd with pearls,
   Thou seem'st, in thy dove-drawn car careering,
Beckoning on, as the swift wheel whirls,
   Thy course thro' that ocean aerial steering,
And my soul would follow and find its nest
In the golden City of Love and Rest.

High on the battlements Arès stands,
   Thy stalwart lover watching and waiting,
Weary of battle and armèd bands,
   Desire of thee in his veins pulsating :—
" Bright and beautiful, come to my breast,
Thou Queen of the City of Love and Rest!"

Hermes, lord of the potent wand,
  By the darksome river the ghosts compelling—
Look! 'Tis the sweep of his glorious hand!—
  Hark to the doom that his lips are telling!—
" Hither! Hither! For life is best
In the golden City of Love and Rest!"

Yonder, Selenè speeds adown
  The dusky slope of the empyrean,
As when in the days of her old renown
  To Latmos she came o'er the isled Ægean,
And to-night Endymion shall be blest
In the golden City of Love and Rest!

O born of the foam of the sheeny sea
  In the sun-lit bay of the land Elysian,
Goddess, again thy star for me
  Unseals in heaven the dazzling vision,
And I would that afar, o'er the waters west,
I had reached that City of Love and Rest.

"THE DEAR OLD FACE."

I saw him in a dream again last night—
  The dear old face, the patient, rayless eyes,
The well-known figure sitting in the light
  In the old chair—and it was no surprise !

Nay, but my soul went out in one great cry
  Of wild rejoicing, to behold him there,
And at his feet I knelt convulsively,
  Fondled his hands, and stroked his soft grey hair ;

" Father, dear father ! is it really you,
  Speak ! ease the doubt that at my heart doth
     ache—
Say that this hour is merciful and true,
  And the stern past a weary, long mistake ! "

One moment—just one moment—did it seem
  He smiled upon me—then my hope was o'er !
But oh, thank God if only in a dream
  I have beheld my life's best friend once more !

"MARGUERITE, FERMEZ LES YEUX."

(From the French.)

Night from her urn on high her poppy-heads lets fall,
Hushed are in ev'ry spot the jarring sounds of day ;
It is the hour when forth the gibbering spectres all
March to invade the gloom and God's behest obey.
Ne'er in the midst of these can conscious Guilt repose,
Their talons in his face they thrust with vengeful cries;
Thou who dost only dream dreams of the pure, white
  rose,
Marguerite, gentle maid, Marguerite, close thine eyes !

Thy days are clouded o'er with bitter thoughts and
  fears,
But to thy soul the night with sweetness doth return ;
By painful labour, thou bread steeped in many tears,
Dost for thy mother old and thy young sister earn.
And yet thou art beloved, and yet thy lot his blest,
And, as to Mary erst, so angels from the skies
Come now, saluting thee, thee as thou slumberest !—
Marguerite, gentle maid, Marguerite, close thine eyes !

Thy chosen of thy love, he who from childhood knew

Thy true heart's constant beat, true to his own heart's
call,

Has joined our soldiers' ranks on shores remote from
view

Oft drenched with blood of France, the noblest blood
of all !—

"Soon will he come again ! "—they tell thee and—
beguile !—

Long since his glorious death his comrades mourned
with sighs !—

Only in dreams henceforth shalt thou behold him
smile !—

Marguerite, gentle maid, Marguerite, close thine eyes!

HOME THROUGH THE STORM.

(An Episode of the North American Blizzard)

The sky is suddenly changed at noon,
  And over the broad expanse
Of prairie and plain, in black array,
  The Storm-king's troops advance,
And the blast of his breath, is as cold as Death
  Piercing and keen as a lance!

The smothering flakes fall fast and thick,
  And cruelly blind the eyes,
And the thundering roar of the terrible wind,
  Strikes down all other cries—
Seems no more hope in this awful world,
  No pity in the skies!

Stumbling along with bewildered steps,
  Teacher and children go,
Through the dark, through the drifts, with eye-balls
    strained
  To catch the home-fire's glow;
And the roar of the terrible wind rolls on,
  And the beating of the snow.

" Teacher—teacher ! we are so cold ! "—
   The little children wail,
But never a sound can reach her ears
   Or in such din avail—
She strives to shelter them all she can,
   Knowing she soon must fail.

Two hundred yards from the sheltering roof,
   Teacher and children rest,
Pale and beautiful, calm and still,
   The little ones clasped to her breast,
And the smile of her marble lips declares
   So dying she has been blest !

Ah, who can doubt that the merciful God
   Guided them on that hour,
Not to the light of an earthly home,
   Where storms and cares must lower,
But into the bliss and warmth and love
   Of His eternal tower?

THE STUDENT OF "THE SCHOOL OF HEART"

Coming home from her painting lesson,
　Coming home as the day declines,
Sweet the smile on her face expectant,
　Bright the light in her eyes that shines.

Stolen meetings are always the nicest ;
　Stolen kisses, they say, the best !
But that's no reason why pretty one loiters—
　She's watching the sun set, of course, in the
　　West !

Whispered words in the gloaming are pleasant ;
　Hands clasp hands in the dusk so well ;
And if an arm round a waist is stealing,
　Who is the wiser ? or, who will tell ?

Coming home from her painting lesson,
　The wind must have faced her up the hill,
For the deep glow of each cheek is spreading,
　The light in her eyes burns brighter still !

Pretty one, pretty one, you have been taking
　(Don't deny it, now, and don't start !)
Just another delightful lesson
　In the old-established " School of Heart " !

THREE PICTURES.

I.

A blue-eyed boy, three summers old,
　　Amid the golden corn
With blood-red poppies in his hands,
　　I met one summer morn.
"God's flowers are beautiful," I said,
　　"God's gifts are everywhere,
But the sweetest flower of all earth's flowers,
　　The fairest gift, is there!"
Stooping down on his brow I placed
　　With reverence a kiss:
A ruined temple of God is man—
　　His shrine unmarred was *this*.
With shy, sweet grace looking up in my face,
　　Gentle and undefiled,
His eyes were bright with the tender light
　　Of Christ the Holy Child!

A stalwart man of fifty years
  I met one autumn day,
His broad, white brow was seamed with cares,
  His hair was iron-grey.

Spent was his life in fever dens
  And haunts of dark despair ;
And none so poor but had cause to bless
  The kind, good doctor there.

Loyal and true to God he stood
  In the midst of vice and sin,
Yet ever, I saw, a fell disease
  Gnawed at his heart within.

But still nor sigh nor fretful cry
  Condemned his Maker's plan ;
His eyes were bright with the steadfast light
  Of Christ the suffering Man !

3.

Late, late, one stormy winter's eve
  In a wretched, fireless room,
On a pallet of straw an old man lay,
  Dying amid the gloom ;

Dying, and yet upon his face
   A smile of joy serene,
For his soul in that its darkest hour
   God's perfect peace had seen.
By his side with sobs a woman knelt
   Who long afar had strayed,
And the father rejoiced, for heard *at last*
   Were the prayers that he had prayed !
So the hand of death was a merciful hand,
   And he bowed beneath the rod,
And his eyes were bright with the deathless light
   Of Christ the loving God !

"FRITZ, LIEBER FRITZ!"

On his camp-bed the Warrior King was lying,
  Never so kingly as on that last day,
And round him, bending o'er the hero dying,
  Friends sadly watched the moments fleet away.

His thoughts recurred to far-off years of gloiy,
  When charging squadrons swept the battle-field,
And the proud Prussian Eagle's talons gory
  Clutched at the prey, and bade Napoleon yield.

Long, long indeed, the vista recollection
  Brought back before the aged Kaiser's glance;
Yet might he see, how by his wise direction,
  A German nation rose confronting France—

How a vast empire was consolidated
  On firm alliances and prescient skill,
And many a risk and peril dissipated
  By his strong servant's overmast'ring will.

Alas!—if only in his brain were stirring,
　　Grand thoughts of triumph!—Hark, that cry of pain,
As if some hand, those blissful memories blurring,
　　Struck at his heart again and yet again!

" Fritz, lieber Fritz!" the dying father, sinking
　　Into the darkness of the realms unknown,
Not of himself but of his son is thinking,
　　His absent son, his best-beloved, his own!

Look! how the feeble hand is stretched out blindly,
　　To grasp one hand—one hand that is not there!
Look! how the eyes seek him, who ever kindly
　　Answered with his their mute, unuttered prayer!

" Fritz, lieber Fritz!"—from noble down to peasant,
　　What heart replied not to the thrilling cry?
Who did not grieve, the son could not be present—
　　Standing that moment his sire's death-bed by?

Ah, but there is who guideth all things for us,
　　God never faltering in His wise decrees!
And it may be when evening closes o'er us,
　　Light shall be shed on sorrows dark as these.

TO "PET."

Sweet, you are all that is gracious,
　　All that is good and true,
And who in your dear eyes gazing,
　　But is lost in their limpid blue !

Sweet, with your tender accents,
　　Sweet, with your winning ways.
You have caught my soul in the meshes
　　Of Love's bewildering rays.

And whether you frown upon me,
　　Or whether my hopes you bless,
I shall only love you the more, love,
　　I can never love you less.

DOWN STREAM ONE SUMMER NIGHT.

The Western wind blows warm to-night,

And not one cloud of fleecy light

Flits like a sail across the main of yon dark
sapphire sky :

In the pale moon's quivering beam

We are drifting down the stream,

My own love, my true love, my little girl and I.

The water ripples at the prow,

Our hearts rejoice to hear it flow,

And 'tis with full content--naught else--that now
and then we sigh ;

Softly reclining, side by side,

Caring not for time or tide,

My own love, my true love, my little girl and I.

On either bank the plaintive note

Of the reed-warbler sounds remote,

And flapping on his leathern wings the dusky bat
goes by ;

Minstrel hear we sweeter still,

Fluting from the copse-crowned hill,

My own love, my true love, my little girl and I.

Oh, that our lives might thus glide on,
With ne'er a grief to brood upon,
We two together, Gladys dear, until the day we die;
In the pale moon's quivering beam,
Calmly drifting down the stream,
My own love, my true love, my little girl and I.

THE NIGHT MY FATHER DIED.

Into the night bewildered,
   Stunned with a dreadful blow
Anguish too great upon me
   For tears, weak tears, to flow,
I staggered purposeless, aimless,
   Only, it seemed, I cried :—
"O God, have pity, have pity !"
   The night my father died.

Bright were the skies above me,
   Bright with ten thousand fires,
Beacons of God that guide men
   To the haven of their desires !
System on system ordered
   By laws that firm abide,
Dazed, I beheld them glowing,
   The night my father died.

Northwards and Southwards and Westwards
   The dazzling watchers stood,
And the voices we hear not were telling
   That all His works are good ;

And Eastwards the mighty Sirius,
   Resplendently panoplied,
Led the armies of God rejoicing,
   The night my father died.

But the stars of the great Orion
   In glory flashed most rare,
Where tower the heavenly ramparts
   And the city lies four-square ;
And, methought that the dear Lord Jesus
   Came forth from its portal wide,
To welcome another pilgrim,
   The night my father died.

O blessed calm of the heavens,
   It fell on my soul like dew !
With a sudden revelation,
   Our loss *his* gain I knew !
Then, wave upon wave within me
   Rose sorrow's surging tide,
And I wept, for my heart was breaking,
   The night my father died.

CONTRASTS.

We turn our honoured Shakespeare's page,
  There, to perfection wrought,
Flashes that instant into view
  Some priceless gem of thought.

In Pope philosophy is found'
  That soars to realms above :
In Burns a limpid stream of song
  Wells from the heart of love.

And Byron's lyric strains are full
  Of passion, force, and fire ;
They rouse us like a clarion's call,
  We feel and we admire !

O barren wastes of modern verse,
  All desolate and chill,
With nothing bright but what ye owe
  To type or binder's skill.

In vain from title-page to close
  Your dulness we explore,
No flashing gems of thought are seen,
  No passion, genius, lore !

Arid, unmeaning epithets,
  Long-winded words sublime,
With here and there a stagnant pool
  Or slough of prurient slime !

So by some sluggish river's marge,
  Amid December gloom,
Look, whilst the chilly mist crawls on,
  For one bright flower in bloom !

So on a dreary reach of sand,
  'Neath skies forlorn and cold,
Out in the harsh north wind all day,
  Search for one grain of gold !

'TWIXT SCYLLA AND CHARYBDIS.

(After Phædrus.)

In the days of Lang Syne, when a man, I opine,
   Might marry two wives or three—
A state of affairs which a Suffolker swears
   They defined as "Polly-gamy!"—

A middle-aged lad two help-meets had,
   One "still on the right side of thirty,"
(So she stated herself), and the other an elf
   Scarcely out of the schoolroom, but flirty.

Now, this middle-aged man, like a badger began,
   In his locks and his beard to betray
Many signs that the snows of Old Age and its woes
   Were not many seasons away.

So wife Number One, as she put it "in fun,"
   And "because it would make him look nice,"
Made a constant attack on the hairs that were black,
   Which her fingers she used as the vice

Then wife Number Two, Number One to out-do,

　That "those horrid white things" might be started

Plucked them out, hair by hair, till the man's pate
　　was bare,

　And his whiskers and beard had departed!

What a rumpus arose!—But at last after blows,

　'Twas agreed, to avoid further pother,

That a white wig he'd wear with his middle-aged dear,

　And a black, when he went with the other.

There's a moral to this, as there commonly is,

　Which away my male readers may carry,

"Grey hairs—quantum suff:!—come to all soon enough

　But you lose all your hair if you marry!

"FORGET-ME-NOTS."

"Forget-me-nots!" I like the sweet old flower,
  With its sweet English name;
Your foreign blooms, that wither in the hour,
  Please not the same.

"Forget-me-nots!" What gift so fair to send,
  What simpler wish could be,
To gentle lady or to loving friend,
  "Think thou of me!"

"Forget-me-nots!" The very name recalls
  Bright summer days gone by,
In meadow valleys, where the water falls
  From crags on high;

And down the glen a silvery runnel gleams
  To join the river's flow,
Along whose banks, like angels seen in dreams,
  These, star-eyed, grow.

" Forget-me-nots ! " Ah, youth's short golden prime,
    Long past with all its joy !
Often I yearn for that serener time,
    No more a boy !

" Forget-me-nots ! " Upon my lowly grave
    Such supplicants appear !
No other mourner for the lost may crave,
    These God will hear !

HOME AGAIN!

June 28th, 1890.

I have come once more to the dear home-land,
 And the City by the sea,
Where every spot is a hallowed shrine
 Of memories dear to me—
The same clear skies, the same old rocks,
 And deep, unfathomed seas,
And the same mysterious charm that lulled
 My young heart into ease.

Here, wandering on by breezy paths,
 High o'er the waters blue,
My life is full of the tenderness
 Of boyhood's days anew,
Or clambering down to the silvery beach
 And dark caves of Carfai,
I hear the cry that the waves declaim
 For ever and for aye.

Ah, to go back and in thought re-live
  That golden summer time,
And list the song of the soaring lark,
  Or the fox-glove's faëry chime!
Their music rang in my ears all day
  And formed my dreams at night—
Was there ever a child, I wonder, who felt,
  Such rapture and delight!

And oh, for the rest and sweet content
  That fills the weary brain,
When the grand cathedral organ sounds
  Its mighty trump again,
And the solemn voices roll and swell
  Along the high-arched nave,
As they tell of the glorious Christian hope
  And the life beyond the grave!

Thank God for the mercy He has shown
  Once more in bringing me
To the dear home-land I love so well,
  And the City by the sea!

Thank God that I have knelt again
In prayer at childhood's shrine,
And known the sweet and happy thoughts
That years ago were mine!

ON HEARING THE CHURCH BELL AT WORMINGFORD TOLLING.

As I sit on the lawn at even,
  The golden sun gone down,
While the glorious colours deepen,
  Rosy and gray and brown ;
Where the white-winged clouds are floating
  Like angels in the blue,
And the dark-green grass and the dusky trees
  Gather a twilight hue,
Over the hill, vibrating still,
  Ringeth a solemn knell,
A long dull toll for a passing soul,
  The moan of the deep Church-bell !

The rooks sail home with a clangour
  Of gladness and delight,
But what of the soul now passing
  Into the infinite ?

Did it part with a sigh from the joyance
  Of earth's sweet summer-tide ?
Or turn from the light to the dark beyond,
  Content and satisfied ?
Over the hill, vibrating still,
  The sad tones fall and swell,
A long dull toll for a passing soul,
  The moan of the deep Church-bell !

O God, is there never a moment
  When these arrows swift and keen
Flash not from the bow of Thy Bowman,
  Unerring and unseen ?
For ever merciless, sateless,
  This bright world must he range,
Strike at the heart whose joy o'erflows,
  Song into wailing change ?
Over the hill, vibrating still,
  Comes the responsive knell—
A long dull toll for a passing soul,
  The moan of the deep Church-bell !

Nay, but the thrush with rapture
  Still flutes her evening song,
And the clarion call of the cuckoo
  The distant hills prolong,
And if "Sorrow and Death!" be the burden
  Of man's most treasured lore,
Those voices tell of a victory
  One day for Life in store,
When never again in grief and pain
  Shall mortal gasp for breath,
Or Church-bell toll for a passing soul,
  Since there is no more Death !

THE LEGEND OF THE FIFTY POUNDER.

"If this true tale believe you won't,
I simply would observe, then, don't!"

Once on a time two fisher folk, they say,
Went fishing on the mere at Wormingford :
From early morning unto dewy eve
They fished and fished and fished, and nothing caught.
All means they tried, all methods of their craft—
Gorged bait and live, snap-tackle—all were vain !
And now the sun gone down, the darkness crept
Over the waters, and a chilly mist
Benumbed the fingers and made blue the nose,
And still they fished and still they nothing caught.
Then spake one fisher to the other there :—
" What profit have we of our labours, friend ?
Vainly we toil ! And night comes on apace,
And lo ! the breeze a fragrant odour wafts
Of rashers frying on the hearth afar,
And buttered toast, and I am faint for food !
Let us go hence, and, comforting our souls

With meat and drink at *The Eight Bells* of Bures,
Go snug to roost, and sleep, and come again,
If needs so be, to-morrow with the morn!"
"Nay, talk not so," replied the other, "stay
Here but a little longer while I make
Yet one more cast with deftly baited hook!
Meantime, despairing one, stand ready thou,
With gaff to help me!—Lo! the rising moon
Floods with her light the surface of the mere,
And, by my halidom, I see—I see—
I see down there—there just beneath that reed—
The biggest pike that ever was, I vow!"

Even as he spake, behold! a mighty rush,
A splash, a foaming of the waters near,
And with one gulp the monster fish had seized
Both bait and hook, and swallowed them, and plunged
Down to its lair that lay so far below!
Hark to the whirring of the reel as fast
And faster still the tough line disappears!
See how the rod, pliant and yielding, bends
But breaks not in the long-continued strain!—
A fight for life!—A fight for victory!—

F

The monster feels the barb—the man the glow
Of coming triumph, and resolves to win!

Warily, cautiously he wound in the line
Around the well-grooved reel, and drew the prey
By slow degrees towards the old black boat!
Forth from the mere at last, at last arose—
In hushed amazement, whilst the fishers gazed—
The head gigantic of a fifty pounder,
Its eyes voracious gleaming ghastly green
In the pale moonbeam.—Ah, what rapture filled
Those fishers' hearts at sight so wonderful!
What thoughts ecstatic surged through either brain
Of fame immortal won by such a catch,
And paragraphs in every sporting print!
How delicately one drew in the line!
How stealthily the other stretched the gaff
To fix it firmly in the monster's gills!
Alas for mortal man and all his schemes!
How like to nothing is his skill at best!
How oft confounded by malicious fate!
Why counts he still his chickens ere they're hatched?
Why cooks he still his fish before he lands 'em?
And otherwise his folly *will* display?

That moment, yes, that very moment when
The sharp points of the sturdy gaff extended
Touched the peculiar orifice whereby
The monster breathed, sudden there rang a cry
Shrill from the midmost waters of the mere,
A cry terrific, terrible, a cry
That issued threatening as from woman's lips :—
" Fishers profane, what do ye with my pike ? "
Down dropped the gaff from this one's nerveless hand,
Away went rod and tackle from the grasp
Of that astonied other, gazing, speechless, awed,
For lo ! upon the waters seemed to burn
A blue and phosphorescent splendour, and,
Clear in the midmost of that eerie light,
The glorious figure of a water-nymph,
" Clothed in white samite, mystic," beautiful,
Stretched forth one arm in menace, dazzling fair !
(The reader can fill in the portrait, to please his or her own
fancy.)

*   *   *   *   *   *   *   *

That night two trembling wretches to a crowd
Of gaping yokels in a village pub
Rehearsed their strange adventure, and, in proof

Thereof, displayed upon the gaff's sharp point,
Still sticking with tenacity most rare,
A grisly portion, a square inch in size,
Torn from the gills of that tremendous fish!

*   *   *   *   *   *   *   *

This is the Legend of the Fishers Twain,
Who saw the Fifty Pounder of the mere
But caught not!—Thousands since have striven
From early morning unto dewy eve
To hook the monster, and to hear the nymph,
But evermore it is their doom, I ween,
Only to see or dream that they have seen!

PISCATOR INFELICISSIMUS.

August, 1890
P.S.—

There are—but they are wicked sceptic wights—
Who not alone "pooh-pooh" the fishers' tale
(True as the tales of fishers always are!)
Anent the pike of such portentous weight,
But also pour contempt and ridicule
Upon the "Vision of the Ladye Faire,"
Saying the light the fishers said they saw

Was but of lucifer that lit a pipe.
Likewise the cry that startled them and lost
The mighty fish, was not of water-nymph,
But rather that of good old Master " Barch,"
The ancient "water-rat," (Alas! He's gone
To fish for "gudgeon" now in Charon's stream!)
Who, objurgating, did address them thus,
With that peculiar snuffle in the nose
Which all who knew him must remember well :—
" What are you arter there, you rascal rogues,
A-usin' Muster Tufflan's fishin'-boat
And poachin' on his waters arter pike
This time o' night?—He never gave you leave
Nor said a ward to me about you!—So
Be off, I tell ye!—And don't never agin
Come fishin' here without you speak to me
Or Muster Tufflan first! Why, bless my soul,
Blarmed if I ever knew sitch impidence
Afore in all my days!—Dashed if I did!"

P. I.

QUO USQUE?

1887.

When shall we wake to sense of dangers deadly ?
   When shall we note how fair occasions fly ?
The Sun of England, is it setting redly,
   A pall of blood its final canopy ?

Nor fleet, nor army capable of guarding
   The mighty borders of a realm so wide ;
No chief like him whose skill was erst retarding,
   At last to crush, the great Napoleon's pride ?

Where are the heroes and the statesmen dauntless,
   To stand for England and her honour now ?
Soon shall her sons be powerless and vauntless—
   Save for that brand of Khartoum on her brow !

O heights of Alma crowned with deathless glory,
   O Balaclava, everlasting name,
Bright is the page ye fill in British story,
   Say, shall it end in cowardice and shame ?

Rise, rise in protest from the shades, each grand one,
   Who bled at Inkerman at duty's call !
Ask :—" Wherefore now, without one blow, abandon
   Those priceless gains for which we dared to fall ? "

Ask :—" Wherefore now should that proud Flag terrific
    Be into darkness and oblivion hurled,
And doomed to cease, on pretexts termed pacific,
    The mighty force that thunder-shook the world ? "

" Soul, take thine ease ! eat, drink thy fill ! be merry ! "
    So saith the heart of England to itself,
Safe in its hold of indolence and very
    Loth to let go one stiver of its pelf !

Ah, that some voice of eloquence and reason
    Might sound amongst us in these latter days,
Showing *that* treason is the basest treason,
    Which, all for self the glorious Past betrays !

The time must come when they who shrink from action,
    Shall face the consequence of duty shirked,
Cursing the might of miserable faction,
    Mourning the ruin which themselves have worked !

Are talents given us only to be wasted ?
    Was Empire gained us only to be lost ?—
Nay, let us rise before shame's cup is tasted
    And England's fortunes hopelessly are crossed !

TEARS:

(From the Greck of Philemon.)

If tears a sovereign remedy

  For life's sore trials were,

And he who wept grew straightway free

  From sorrow and despair,

Who would not, so this rule might hold,

Buy tears at any price in gold?

THE ROCK OF BOIA.

I stood on the Rock of Boia
  One evening last July,
With joy the marvel beholding
  Of land and sea and sky.

The Rock of Boia the Chieftain,
  His camp you trace there now,
And the signs of an ancient people
  Are stamped upon its brow.

Before me the hills of Ramsey
  Shone clear in the sunset's ray,
And the deep blue waters sparkled
  Outside Porthlisci Bay.

Cornfield and pasture and moorland
  Beneath me I descried,
And the valley where winds the Alan,
  And the broad expanse of St. Bride,

And out of the great Atlantic,
　As if they rode a race,
The white "sea-horses" rushing
　In triumph into Porthclais.

There fancy brought before me
　Visions and scenes of old
In the far-off times of Demetia,
　By no historian told,

But only in faery legend
　Or fragment of bardic lay,
Shrined like a sacred treasure,
　And kept unto this day.

Here Gavran, perchance, stood gazing,
　Ere his galleys sailed in quest
Of the green Isles of Enchantment,
　Far out at sea to the west,

And saw their grassy hillocks,
　And their rich luxuriant meads,
And the great black cattle plashing
　Thro' Avalon's rills and reeds.

And here was there battle and bloodshed
   And the dying Brython's groan,
Long ere to Gurmarc's faith was raised
   The cross-engraven stone.

And here did the good Saint Dewi
   With Boia the heathen fight,
When forth from Parc-y-Castell
   He marched in Christ's own might.

And the gods of the Gäel waxed feeble,
   And Dunawel's hair in vain
In the hazel-grove was braided,
   And the fair, young victim slain.

Ah, changes and revolutions
   Wrought in the restless years,
Leaving behind you so little
   To mark men's hopes or fears!

A name on some lonely headland,
   A tale that with wondrous spell
Still clings to some lichened boulder,
   Still hallows some limpid well,

And stirs in the heart of the hearer
  Emotions strange and wild,
As in the ear of an old man,
  The song he loved when a child.

Say, is this feeling remembrance
  Of some preceding life,
When in other form we were present
  And shared in Being's strife?

Or an old, time-faded picture,
  Or tapestry of the brain,
From sire to son transmitted,
  No longer clear and plain?

" Legends and superstitions
  Of the darkest times!"—we say,
But what of ourselves, when the ages
  Have whirled our dust away?

Will the after generations
  Our names and deeds recall?
Or only in deeper darkness
  Oblivion shroud us all?

Ah, folly of man's ambition!
　Ah, vanity of his schemes,
Building on shadowy bases
　His unsubstantial dreams!

Pass hence, O perishing mortals!
　There is nothing on earth abides
But the Love of Christ for ever—
　In Him the heart confides!

1892.

THE SCENT OF THE BEAN IN BLOOM.

Time takes much, but it cannot rob me
   Yet of the joy with the summer born,
Still with rapture the woodland fills me,
   And the tender green of the growing corn.
My heart, as the blood in my veins throbs faster,
   Beats to a wild, exultant tune,
And oh for the scent of the sweet bean-blossom
   Stealing over the fields in June!

Joy for the presence of God's fair children,
   Pure white lilies and roses red,
Lilac, laburnum, pink thorn and may-bloom,
   And the chestnut burgeoning overhead!
Joy for the sunlight flooding the landscape,
   Joy for the silvery sheen of the moon,
And joy for the scent of the sweet bean-blossom
   Stealing over the fields in June!

Time takes much, but it cannot alter
   Some dear memories of the past ;
A look, a sigh, or a word low-spoken—
   All else may perish—still live and last.
And ev'n on the verge of our day's declining
   Back to our lost youth's ardent noon,
We are borne on the scent of the sweet bean-blossom
   Stealing over the fields in June!

Earth is beautiful, God is gracious,
   Ever a Father's loving care
Guides the steps of His mortal children,
   Breathes its balm in the summer air.
Lift your hearts to the heavens above you!
   Take, rejoicing, life's perfect boon,
Glad for the scent of the sweet bean-blossom
   Stealing over the fields in June!

A SKETCH.

He banged the table with his fist,
    And snorted out a speech,
And sometimes would his voice arise,
    In incoherent screech ;
His view of History was queer
    And not at all exact—
The sort of thing so often found
    In Liberation tract !
His code of morals, sooth to say,
    Had made Bill Sikes elate,
For from his decalogue he struck
    Commandment Number Eight !
The Parson and the Church alike
    He loathed and held in scorn,
Because the twain his long abuse
    Too patiently had borne !
To pay just debts he did maintain
    Was hardship worse than death,
And on this theme from morn till night
    Expended all his breath.

He saw no good in any thing
   Except his own sweet fad,
And, if in other matters sane,
   O'er one at least went mad.
Poor man! His only aim in life,
   Pursued with eager zest,
Was, while unbested *he* remained,
   The Clergyman to best!

A LEGEND OF ST. SIMON'S SKULL.

"Nihil credibilius quam incredibile."

At Saint Gregory's Church in a certain town,
 "Recessed" in the vestry wall
Is the skull of a Saint—of some renown,
 Or he wouldn't be there at all!

Once an archbishop, he lost his head
 In the turbulent days of yore,
(So the best of us do in a season of dread!)
 And never could find it more.

But somebody must have picked it up,
 And placed it long ago
In its glazed recess in the vestry wall,
 Or it wouldn't be there, you know!

Into that church I wandered one day,
  From cares to seek a lull,
And I managed, before I went away,
  A peep at Saint Simon's skull.

Well, a skull is a skull, and never a sight
  One wishes long to see,
Not calculated to cause delight
  Whatever the skull may be!

But it set me a-thinking, because it seemed
  So tiny a skull in size,
Not the sort of casket that I had deemed
  An episcopal soul would prize!

Said I to myself:—Saint Simon, you
  No doubt were a Prince of the church
And well, in your day, to wield you knew
  The Cantuarensian birch.

Better, perhaps, than His Grace who now
  Sits in your vacant chair!—
Yet, pardon me, Sir, but you must allow
  What a very small skull you were!"

From that glazed recess in the vestry wall
    Came an angry snarl to my ear:
"The curse of the dead upon you fall!
    Is there nothing which you revere?

How dare you stare in a manner so rude,
    And with thoughts much ruder still,
In the teeth of a saint by far too good
    This dusty old box to fill?

But both alike are you and your age,
    Who put me here for a show,
While *my* position on history's page
    Not two in a million know!"

"A cat may look at a king, my lord!
    That saying you can't annul!
Much more may a presbyter of the church
    Examine a bishop's skull!

I am sorry for you, Saint Simon, too,
    For it seems that *where you are*,
The tempers and ways of folks in these days
    Are worse than ours by far!

Indeed, such passion as you have shown
    At an innocent remark,
Goes far to prove that your grace don't own
    Of saintship a single spark !

Nay, the terrible doubt occurs to me
    As I gaze at your outline dull :
' Is it perfectly sure that the skull you see
    Is the real Saint Simon's skull ? ' "

Rattled the bones of that grisly head,
    As stirred by impotent spleen,
And the hiss of a malediction sped
    Whence erst the lips had been.

" Anathema maranatha !— Beast !
    Your soul as sure as fate,
If you don't go down on your knees at least,
    I'll excommunicate ! "

" Alas ! such language confirms my doubt,
    For Simon the Saint was good
And died absolving the rabble rout
    Who thirsted for his blood !

Then in Saint Gregory's church were heard
  Mysterious sounds of awe,
For the skull bounced up to the top of the box,
  And a tooth dropped out of its jaw!

" If I only could get from this glass case,"
  It shrieked, "upon my life
I'd teach you, Sir, to insult to her face
  The great Wat Tyler's wife!"

"GOOD NIGHT! GOOD BYE!"

"Good night! good bye!"—Dear, at the door you
    stand,

And with soft fingers lightly touch my hand;

Within, the firelight's scintillating glow

Around your form a silvery sheen doth throw,

And I—am lost! In vain, with yearning eyes,

I look in yours for tender, sweet replies:

I only see unaltered mien and hue,

That calm good-humour which seems part of you.

"Good night! good bye!" our ways lie wide apart;

Youth, Hope are yours, but I, with aching heart,

Into the dark go forth, as now I go;

'Good night! good bye!" maybe 'tis better so.

LLECHLAWER, OR THE TALKING STONE.

In days of old at St. David's
  A white slab spanned the brook,
Worn smooth by the feet of pilgrims
  Their course that way who took.

Decided objections had it
  That a corpse should cross thereby ;
And one day, expressing abhorrence,
  It cracked itself with a cry !

(So at least says *Giraldus Cambrensis*
  Whom I see no reason to doubt,
For to judge by his manifold writings
  He knew his way about.)

Now a prophecy of Merlin
  Concerning that slab was shown :—
" Let the Man who shall conquer Ireland
  Beware of the Talking Stone."

King Henry, Rosamund's lover,
   Came, so the story goes,
To that spot, and, in safety crossing,
   Turned up his royal nose :—

" I have come from conquering Ireland
   (This morning to be exact) !
I have crossed and no evil has happened !
   Your stone and your prophet are cracked ! "

But what if the wisdom of Merlin
   Was quite misunderstood,
And he never referred to Llechlawer,
   As he probably never would ?

What if his prescience warned us,
   Who dwell in these latter days,
Of a Talking *Stone* who on Irish themes
   Is *glad* to be cracked always ?

BY THE WATER MILL, 1891.

The waters flow, the waters flow
So gaily in the vale below,
The mill-wheel with incessant sound
Goes ever whirling, whirling round ;
The bees are humming blithe and free
About the fragrant linden-tree,
And glad the swallows' frequent cry
Against the blue of yonder sky.

The waters flow, the waters flow
I wonder where the wanderers go,
Past purple loosestrife, lily star
And all the pleasant shapes that are
Reflected in the lucent cool
Of each sequestered, secret pool,
And what the wondrous tale they tell
In liquid murmurings so well !

The waters flow, the waters flow
Like voices whispering soft and low,
Of love and life and all the bliss
That in this world concentred is ;
No jarring sound the spell to break,
No pain, no sorrow, no heart-ache,
I listen, listen, and my breast
Drinks in tranquillity and rest.

The waters flow, the waters flow
So gaily in the vale below,
The mill-wheel with incessant sound
Goes ever whirling, whirling round ;
The bees are humming blithe and free
About the fragrant linden tree,
And all day long the sunlight falls
Upon the miller's orchard walls.

THE STRAITS OF THE PERSIAN CAT

(A Tale in Rhyme).

A Persian Cat so sleek and gray
Went forth to see the world one day,
He travelled far, he travelled fast
And reached St. Petersburg at last.
His wily friend, the Russian Bear,
Received him very kindly there,
Took him the rounds—to dinners, teas,
To balls, receptions, routs, levees,
Then, parting, with emphatic paws
Showed him his muzzle, teeth and claws,
And whispered : "O my Persian Cat
Elsewhere be careful what you're at !
Don't listen to the Lion's flam
Or else I'll squeeze you into jam !"

The Persian Cat, perplexed, afraid,
His journey next to Berlin made ;
The triple-headed Eagle there
Received him with a gracious air
Asked him how long he meant to stay—
What business urged him come that way ?
Then said, "Good-bye," remarking, " Be
Cautious, dear sir, of thwarting *me !* "

Thence, o'er the sea the Persian Cat
Passed, whilst his heart went pit-a-pat
Until he reached the white-cliffed strand
Of the great British Lion's land :
In London town that noble beast
Prepared his guest a sumptuous feast,
Trotted him out in Park and Row
And took him down to Windsor Show,
Introduced the monkeys at the Zoo,
Likewise those at St. Stephen's too,
Gave him Sir Drummond Wolff as valet
And organised a special ballet
All for his pleasure and delight
At Drury Lane on Sunday night ;
Then sent him home to Ispahan
With such dispatch as lions can,
Growling : " Adieu, my friend !—Beware
Don't chum, old chappie, with that Bear !"

Doleful, the Persian Cat departed
In sore distress and heavy-hearted,
Pondering the fate of those that be
Betwixt the d-v-l and deep sea !

MORFA RHUDDLAN.

Who shall break the peaceful slumbers
  Of the native harp to tell
How, o'erborne by countless numbers,
  Caradoc the glorious fell?

Hark! a voice in accents wailing
  Sings, to sad and plaintive chords,
How the might of freemen failing
  Broke before the Mercian hordes,

When the Marsh of Rhuddlan weltered
  With the blood of warriors brave,
And nor rock nor forest sheltered
  Those who fled the vengeful wave.

Ah, that place of death and slaughter!
  Thousands did the spear consume,
Thousands more the angry water
  Swept remorseless to their doom.

See them on the red plain lying,
　In their eyes hate's changeless glare,
Briton, Saxon, dead and dying,
　Horribly commingled there!

Weep, ye maidens, for your brothers,
　Howl, ye widows of a day,
Mourn your sons, heart-broken mothers,
　Smitten in the fatal fray!

Woe to lover! woe to marrow
　Fallen by a blow accurst!
Battle-axe and sword and arrow
　Wrought indeed their very worst!

Who is this that lieth senseless,
　Ghastly in the pale moonbeam,
Power from a hand defenceless
　Past or passing, like a dream?

Bodies piled around him, savage
　Mercians whom his right hand slew,
Wrathful that they came to ravage
　Cambria's plains and mountains blue?

Caradoc the king has perished !
  Caradoc the great is dead !
O ye people, whom he cherished,
  Wail for him and bow the head !

Make ye bitter lamentation,
  Curse the fray on Rhuddlan plain,
Where the darling of the nation
  By the paynim wolves was slain !

Yet, oh yet, if not victorious,
  (This with pride at least forth tell)
Not dishonoured, not inglorious,
  There the British chieftain fell !

Yonder on his false gods calling—
  But in vain !—fierce Offa lies,
While eternal night is falling
  On his fixed and glazing eyes !

Deadly was the blow delivered
  At the glory of our land,
But the rock of Freedom shivered
  To the hilt the tyrant's brand !

And the Christ, for Whom contending
　　Thousands freely died that day,
Soon, our bitter trials ending,
　　Over Mercia stretched His sway !

Morfa Rhuddlan, sad the story
　　Which the mournful bard recalls
While the dirge of doom and glory
　　Plaintive from the harp-string falls.

Yet, methinks, that those who love her,
　　E'en in chords that wail her shame,
Can for Wales at least discover
　　Tones of never-dying fame !

FROM "THE CUPS." COLCHESTER.

A barrel-organ grinding out an air;
  A troop of girls and gamins in the street,
Gathered with "gentle" language and fixed stare
  A poor relation from the South to greet:

Dragged by a chain where'er his master goes,
  A masquerade in miniature of man,
His face a picture of unuttered woes,
  He lives, not as he would but as he can.

What is he thinking of?—The race that came
  Somehow as mankind from his own to be?—
Tush! 'Tis not so, but—who the thought can blame?—
  "This mouldy biscuit's not the food for me!"

Starved, shivering wretch! Doomed thus in chills and
    fears
  To gambol for the sport of gaping elves!
Bring them a mirror!—Now, my human dears,
  Study the sweet reflection of yourselves!

Ev'n at St. Stephen's you, perchance, might see
    As quaint grimace or hear as fine a screech
In *some* who claim yon antic's kin to be,
    Barring the tail and lack of thumb and speech.

There is a moral in these rhymes of mine,
    Perhaps a parallel may, too, be found,
Unhappy beast, with that estate of thine
    In lives which should with higher aims be crowned.

Our barrel-organ is the School Board bane,
    Its stale old tune for ever grinding out,
Our monkeys, infants, tied to Drudgery's chain,
    A spectacle for gods and men, no doubt!

Our mouldy biscuit is the Christless food
    Fanatics fling them for the soul's support:
Their proper sustenance the bigot brood
    Long since denied or the supplies cut short!

Dull haunts of Torture, where we teach the child
    Tricks in "Three R.'s" and matters just as rare!
Far happier, little ape, if sporting wild
    In some deep forest with his "brother" there!

Warped from their natural growth are child and brute,
  Forced to keep time with that unending tune,
In either case a life that bears no fruit
  But that of misery or death too soon!

In either case, by man's blind ignorance
  Heaven's wise decree and order set aside,
Short space upon earth's stage the mimics prance
  Where health and freedom are alike denied!

Let each return to his true sphere and clime,
  Those happy homes which God's blest sunlight warms!
And hence—no doubt we'll bear the loss in time!—
  With your false system and the prigs it forms!

THE VARIETY OF IT.

Scorchingly hot is the wind in June,
    Blazing suns in the sky,
And oh ! in our tight black clothes compressed,
    For cooling drinks we sigh !
The leaves all droop, and the pale flowers fade,
The thermometer's 90° in the shade !

Bitterly cold is the wind in June,
    Thunder, and floods, and hail,
And we shiver and shake in our summer suits,
    And at night we drink mulled ale !
And, sciatica gnawing at each hip-joint,
The thermometer's down to freezing point !

Cloudlessly blue are the skies in June
    For part of a week or a day !
" How lovely the country is looking now—
    Summer is come," we say ;
And down to the river or down to the sea
Hies many a jovial company.

Horribly black are the skies in June
  For the rest of the time, and rain
Pours, and pours, and pours, and pours,
  Deluging valley and plain,
And alas ! Alack ! and wellaway !
For the year's Whitsun Holiday !

THE COW WITH THE WOODEN LEG.

'Tis the time of the big, big mushroom and
   The monstrous turnip too,
And our old Sea-serpent friend in print
   Reveals a coil or two.
Many a fanciful mind now lays
   In its own mare's nest an egg,
But the thing that tickles my fancy most
   Is " the Cow with the Wooden Leg ! "

This must be the animal of that ilk
   Who, in childhood's trustful noon
We were taught to believe by our rev'rend sires,
   For joy "jumped over the moon ! "
If you doubt her existence, to Yorkshire wolds
   An excursion make, I beg,
For somewhere there, I forget quite where
   Is " the Cow with the Wooden Leg ! "

I would also remark that it seems to me
　A matter for further search,
And one which the curious in such things
　Should not leave in the lurch,
Whether "the cow with the iron tail,"
　Whose "milk" fills many a keg,
Be mother or sister or cousin or aunt
　To "the Cow with the Wooden Leg!"

BERCEUSE.

(From the French).

As with the dawn a fisher hastens forth
And scans intent east, west, and south and north,
A day serene forecasting from the sky,
Thy mother, child, dreams of thy destiny !
Angel from heaven, what wilt thou be on earth ?
A man of peace ?—or warrior scorning mirth ?
A tonsured priest ?—or gallant knight at ball ?
Or brilliant bard ?—grand speaker ?—General ?
     Waiting till then, these knees upon,
     My blue-eyed cherub, slumber on !

His looks declare he's born for "derring do !"
O laurel wreaths how proud I'll be of you !
A soldier ? Nay !—This is a general here !
He speeds ! He flies !—Field-marshall, ho ! appear !
Behold him now, where swells the conflict high,
With radiant front the storm of shot defy !
The foemen turn !—all to his valour yield !
Blow bugles blow ! my son has won the field !
     Waiting till then, these knees upon,
     Heroic victor, slumber on !

Not so, my child!—the thought my soul alarms,—
I fear for thee the blood stained play of arms—
Rather live thou in some calm home of prayer,
From dangers kept, beneath God's watchful care,
Be thou this lamp enkindled at the shrine
Of fervent faith, and may this breath of thine,
Like incense sweet by seraphs offered, rise,
What time they hymn th' Eternal, to the skies!

    Waiting till then, these knees upon,
    My fair young Levite, slumber on!

Forgive, O God, a fond heart's foolish hope,
For I saw not Thy wise laws wondrous scope!
If I have sinned, Oh punish only me
For I alone have lost my faith in Thee!
Even beside the cradle of her boy
Prayer should alone a mother's thoughts employ,
Deign for my child to choose, O God, and bless—
Far more than I Thou seest, and lov'st not less!

    Waiting till then, these knees upon,
    My blue-eyed cherub, slumber on!

THE TRYSTING-PLACE.

Alone at dusk in the woodland glade
She lingers where the palisade
That girds the Chase is broken down,
Hard by the path to Stanmore town.
What brings the Lady Delia there
Time after time with expectant air?
What makes her eyes so brightly shine,
A blush her cheeks incarnadine?

> Listen! Listen!—Her blue eyes glisten!
> Oh, the rapture where fond hearts meet!
> Stolen pleasures are richest treasures!
> Stolen kisses are doubly sweet!

A patter of feet on the fallen leaves
And with joy tumultuous her bosom heaves!
A bar or two of an old love-song—
She knows, she knows who is speeding along!
Oh, Digby Gray is poor, they say,
And the earl, her father, is proud and stern,
But love, you know, will find a way
To serve somehow a young man's turn!

> Listen! Listen!—Her blue eyes glisten!
> Oh, the rapture when fond hearts meet!
> Stolen pleasures are richest treasures!
> Stolen kisses are doubly sweet!

TO HESPER.

Out of thy pearly shell,
Star, that arising
In beauty transcendent
Gleamest resplendent
Far o'er the waves of the orient sea,
Falters my tongue to tell
The rapture surprising,
The bliss that is rarest,
Deity fairest,
Stirred in my heart by the vision of thee!
Daughter of Eos,
Down from thy shoulders,
Dazing beholders,
Thy long golden ringlets dishevelled are flowing
As when from a mountain
A bright, crystal fountain
Falls sheer, like a diamond flashing and glowing!
Star of the dawning,
Herald of light
Welcome, thrice blessed one
Banishing night!

A STRIKING AGE.

I do conclude, and I defy
   The world to contradict me,
That this is more a striking age
   Than when at school they licked me !

The soldiers strike, the bobbies strike.
   Tho' sworn the peace to keep it,
The gas men strike, the dockers strike,
   And as they sow they reap it !

From kings to cads the human race
   An attitude is striking,
The more *bizarre*, the more absurd,
   The better to their liking !

We've striking scenes upon the stage,
   And sometimes in the boxes,
When critic gents and bards engage
   In fisticuffian " knockses."

What striking language oft we hear
  From Irish patriots pouring,
As if their own unnumbered bulls
  Were all at once a-roaring !

M'yes ! I do conclude from this
  Our ancestors were Vikings,
They always came to blows—and *we*
  Are always at our strikings.

IN MEMORIAM

There is no task however lowly,
  There is no rank however mean,
But is made beautiful and holy
  By fellowship with things unseen.

Lives spent Christ-like yet unregarded,
  Days passed in doing silent good,
By a just Judge shall be rewarded,
  By whom all hearts are understood.

If for this world we laboured only,
  Then were our lot unfair indeed—
Here, worn with sorrows, tortured, lonely—
  There, night unending, Virtue's meed !

Such is the faith that sceptics cherish,
  Such is the future *they* conceive,
Who at the grave will sooner " perish "
  Than in the life beyond believe.

But God be thanked for hopes more glorious,
   And noble thoughts in Christ made sure,
By which we rise o'er doubt victorious
   And for His sake all things endure !

So, "earth to earth," but unrepining,
   With words of comfort not despair,
We lay thee, friend, whose soul is shining,
   In that eternal radiance *there !*

THE PATTISWICK CLUB.

November 30th, 1886.

In Pattiswick did twenty-five
  Poor labourers agree
To form a little Friendly Club,
  "For benefit to we."
Their contributions in a bag,
  And that inside a box
They carefully bestowed, not locked
  With one of Chubbs's locks,
But with an ordinary sort
  Such as you often see,
The wards of which will kindly fit,
  Well, any sort of key !
The box beneath a member's bed
  Was next securely put—
I dare say one or other gave
  "A shove to 't wi' his foot !"
Then to another's custody
  The key they did convey,
And homeward all exulting went
  Right merrily away.

I

The bag was safe, the box was safe,
  The key was safe likewise !
" Yes, safe as in the Bank," thought Hodge,
  " My sick allowance lies ! "
Alas ! Alas ! Last week they went
  Instalment for to draw,
Opened the box, untied the bag—
  One florin in they saw !
Now Pattiswick's bucolic cots
  Resound with cries of grief,
Because its bumpkins failed to make
  " Allowance " for a thief !

A CLOUDLESS SKY.

A cloudless sky, and not a breath of air
  To waft the dead leaves softly to their graves ;
A strange deep silence broken only where
  The slumberous ocean, hushed its giant waves,
Heaves with the tiniest ripple to the shore,
Its wrath of yesterday forgot, and stilled the tempest's
    roar.

A cloudless sky, straight to whose dome serene
  The blue smoke from a lowly hut ascends,
And by the door, as fair as any queen,
  Her father's net the fisher maiden mends,
And to herself, as softly as may be,
Sings of her love, far, far away, her sailor on the sea.

A cloudless sky ! ah, well for us indeed,
  That sometimes when our lives are all too bright,
And hours of joy to hours of joy succeed,
  God veils the future in such dazzling light,
That not to know it, is life's greatest boon !—
Sing softly of your love, fair maid, dark sorrow cometh
    soon.

He sleeps upon a couch of ruby red
 In the cool alcove of a merman's hall,
A dreamless sleep, a sleep from which, 'tis said,
 None ever woke, or may awake at all,
And by his side unutterable things,
Combing her yellow hair the while, the merman's
  daughter sings.

WANTED—LEADERS OF THE PEOPLE.

We are only a mob who jostle and push
  In a feverish sort of strife
(Some call it "progress" but Heavens knows where!
  Some style it "seeing life!")

We tread on our neighbour's toes and dig
  Our elbows into his side,
And we seldom or never his pardon ask,
  For that's to stoop our pride!

We are brave by fits when the sun shines fair,
  But oftener act the sneak,
And if none cries "Shame!" it is ten to one
  But we trample to death the weak!

And there's none to warn us and none to teach—
  No guidance now men find—
But the multitude leads the van these days
  And the leaders lag behind.

Or sit on a wall in a cautious mood,
　In dread of a fall or bump,
To see which side, as they phrase the thing,
　" The cat intends to jump! "

True! a glib address and a crafty smile
　Will always take us in,
Especially if the owner's known
　To be well supplied with " tin."

And we usually find him out too late,
　And groan when the mischief's done,
Then seek his like, to be diddled again
　And again, each mother's son!

Bah! Leaders of men in the olden days
　Were leaders worth their salt,
Not like our modern invertebrates,
　The blind, the lame, the halt!

They went before—*they* led the way,
　Dauntless and wise and true!
Are there any survivors of the race?
　I know of none—do you?

AN EXPLANATION.

September 23rd, 1889.

Saturn and Mars,
Two baleful stars,
Last week hob-nobbed together ;
The skies were bright,
And clear the night,
Unclouded autumn weather!

Long years had passed
Since they held last
A close confabulation ;
Long years away
Must speed ere they
Might meet in consultation.

On earth men feared,
As they two neared,
Weak hearts with terrors trembling,
And pale nymphs sighed,
" Ah, woes betide
From planets thus assembling !"

Some shook their heads,
Expecting dreads
To fall upon them thickly ;
" Boulanger's end
The stars portend,
Or rise to power more quickly !"

Some said "It meant
A sad event—
The death of King or Kaiser !"
Some thought, "May be,
We soon shall see
A Red Republic Blazer !"

Some cried, "We know
To England woe
That sign betokens plainly !
Rads shall beat down
Both Church and Crown,
The Blues resisting vainly !"

Voices of doom,
A tale of gloom
Proclaimed in accents frantic :
"Volcanic shocks !
Enormous rocks
Barring the whole Atlantic !"

Dionè sly
Stood, twinkling, by,
Selenè fair beside her,
To Terra they
Contrived to say
No evil should betide her!

And then, to me,
In tones of glee,
The foam-born goddess, smiling,
Spake sweet and low,
As long ago
When my young heart beguiling :

" Wiseacres all
Attention call
To this and that and 'tother ;
To prove them wrong,
Go write this song,
Explaining thus their pother :

"To Saturn old,
Mars brave and bold
(Pray more attentive be, Sir!)
Came, purchasing
His brightest ring,
A birthday gift for *me*, Sir !"

ONE JUNE DAY AND NOW.

1886

The sunshine glare on the level road
 Where the hedge affords no shade,
The stir of the breeze in the leafy trees,
 The hum by the wild bee made,
The fragrance borne from the bean-field near, ·
 I feel and hear and see
Fresh and gay as the summer day
 When Jack was last with me.

I was waiting for him—I mind it well
 That golden afternoon,
And oh, the bliss of a lover's kiss
 When he came but not too soon!
Where is he now?—O life, O love,
 Too quickly clouded o'er!
Summer may come to her last year's home,
 But the dead return no more!

He lies far off in the wild Soudan
    White faced with folded hands—
The warm life-blood from his heart which flowed
    Quaffed by the savage sands!
He died that the cowards who ruled this realm
    Might still to office cling,
For what recked they of the deadly fray
    Or the mourner sorrowing?

Ah, never along the level road,
    Sweetheart, you come again,
I wait and wait by the trysting gate,
    But now I wait in vain!
No more the stir and the joy of June
    Can wake glad thoughts in me:
My summer is sped, my hope lies dead
    With Jack beyond the sea!

THE HAUNTED BARN.

A gnarled wych-elm, a pollard oak,
  And rank black alders front the scene ;
Hard by, a pond where seethes unbroke
  A loathsome scum of slimy green ;
A smell of damp and of decay,
And toad-stools mouldering away.

With broken walls and rotting doors,
  That scarce are held by bolt or hinge,
With moss-grown thatch, and lichened shores,
  And chinks which dusty cobwebs fringe,
The old Barn seems to stand and mourn
For years that never will return.

By day its lonely gloom is stirred
  But seldom. Comes to gaze thereat
At times a solitary bird,
  At times a weasel or a rat,
Who, doubtful of the silence there,
Soon flies affrighted to his lair.

At dusk, the grisly owl is seen
   To circle slowly round its eaves,
And the wych-elm, as if in teen,
   Sighs drearily through all its leaves,
While the black alders whisper low
The secret of some awful woe.

But never, down the rutted lane
   That leads you to this spot forlorn,
Comes lumbering the farmer's wain
   Beneath a weight of hay or corn :
Bad luck with cares would seam *his* face
Who stored his crop in such a place !

No peasant loves to pass that way
   When twilight darkens into night,
For one, more venturesome, they say,
   Saw once a strange, unearthly sight—
A girl, in sheeny garments drest,
Hands clasped in anguish on her breast.

She passed him as the gate he neared,
   There was no sound of footsteps there,
Only it seemed as if he heard

The low sad wailing of despair !
Towards the pond he marked her glide,
To vanish as she reached its side !

Now long ago, as old folks tell,
    When France and England fought at sea,
Up at the Holt, one day it fell,
    Sad news was brought to Farmer Lee—
It drove with grief the old man wild—
The French had killed his only child !

And Margery, the orphan maid
    Whom Parson Gray had ta'en and reared,
From that day forward, it is said,
    Inexplicably disappeared,
And though they sought her high and low
Her fate none knew, or e'er will know.

But since that day ('tis doubtful why)
    The lonely barn became accurst,
And in broad day, to hurry by,
    Was all the very bravest durst,
Since ever in their thoughts they had
Pale Margery and a sailor lad !

MRS. SILVAN EVANS.

Death, hast thou no compassion? Must thy dart
  For ever speed to suit a cruel mood?
How else from earth so suddenly depart
  The gentle and the good?

Ah, light of eyes for ever lost in gloom!
  Gone mother, sister, daughter, loving wife!
Who hath not quailed before this awful doom
  Some season in his life?

Who hath not mourned some day the vacant place
  In the bright circle gathered at his hearth—
Missed *one* gay laugh or yearned to see *one* face
  More than all others worth?

Who hath not longed, left utterly alone
  In the cold world to battle with his pain,
For *one* soft touch or *one* familiar tone?
  And longed alas! in vain.

So now. Dark Death hath taken one whose loss
  Words are too weak for those who loved to tell—
One who taught others as she bore her cross
  Their own to bear as well!

One who in blameless innocence of life
    Along the world's bewildering path could roam ;
The fondest mother and the sweetest wife
    That ever blessed a home !

The poor lament a true and generous friend,
    The sick a comforter, and all a guide
Before whose gentleness crabbed Age would bend,
    In whom the young confide.

Beside her grave all classes, all degrees,
    Paid the last tribute of deserved respect,
And stooping down on reverential knees
    Her bier with flowers bedecked.

Another mound beneath that sombre yew
    Tells the sad story of this world again—
O friends ! to whom my heart's best aid is due,
    How shall I soothe your pain ?

I cannot pen the cold and formal phrase
    Of idle consolation ! Hope is fled !
Who holds the clue to life's dark, tangled maze,
    God keep you and the dead !

SPRING, AND THE SONG OF THE NIGHTINGALE.

God sends His angel every year
  With power from on high :
He rolls the stone from the sepulchre
  Where all things silent lie,
And wakes to life with a whispered word
  Blossom, and blade, and spray—
There is light in the East, there is hope in
    the breast—
  Winter hath passed away !

God sends His angel every year
  With a song for souls to learn ;
Not with the flashing of golden wings
  Or the fiery wheels that burn
This messenger of love descends,
  Nor with Æolian shell—
Hark ! The sweet low note of a bird, remote
  In the moon-lit hazel dell !

K

Come to our hearts, angelic Spring,
  And roll all doubts away!
Sing on, mysterious Voice of the night,
  Thy strange, unearthly lay!
We are weary, and often over our world
  Sorrow its shadow casts—
Point to the Life no winter kills,
  Sing of the Love that lasts!

A PERFECT DAY IN JUNE.

The warm wind rushing ever
 Afar from the western sea,
The shadowy heat-haze hanging
 Low upon lawn and lea,
The clouds in fantastic fleeces
 Dotting the azure mead—
Oh, joy for the rapture of living
 This perfect day indeed !

Not yet are the trees full-foliaged
 In tenderest shades of green,
Not yet in rich plenty of blossom
 Is the rose on the south wall seen ;
But the may with the lilac is vying,
 And Veronica bids " good-speed "
From each bend of the road as we journey :
 'Tis a perfect day indeed !

Carols the thrush in the garden,
  Answers the merle on the hill,
Chaffinch and linnet and goldfinch
  Piping it merrily still :
Jubilant voices of nature
  God-ward our thoughts to lead,
Till our hearts overflow with the blessing
  Of this perfect day indeed !

Joy for the blaze of the golden
  Buttercups o'er the lea,
Joy for the warm wind rushing
  Soft from the western sea,
Joy for the river reaches
  Flashing by fallow and mead,
Joy for the sense of existence
  This perfect day indeed !

A WELCOME REPRIEVE

Hurrah for the coming of August,
  When we bid adieu to the streets,
And away to the moors and mountains
  Where the flashing torrent fleets !
Hurrah for the sense of freedom
  Untrammelled, unconfined,
As we leave the smoke and din of town
  A hundred miles behind !

Away to the lochs in the Highlands,
  Or the beautiful bays of the West,
Where the broad and blue Atlantic
  Invites to its heaving breast ;
Or where, in some glen sequestered
  Of brackened boulders cool,
Lies, waiting the rod of the angler,
  The trout's most favoured pool !

Hurrah for the water-parties
　Down moon-lit rural stream,
Past farm, and mill, and meadow,
　And mere chock-full of bream,
With the smell of the ripening barley
　Fresh on the sweet night-breeze,
And the cry of the churn-owl calling
　From the hollow churchyard trees !

Hurrah for the sands of the sea-shore,
　Or a blow on the Norfolk Broads,
Better than all this feverish whirl
　Of the worship of London's gods !
Better than all the jangle
　Of politics and creeds—
Thank Heaven that after the Season
　A breathing space succeeds !

NEW YEAR'S EVE, 1887.

Turn the glass, for the sands, exhausted,
  Run no more, and the year must die!
Toll the bell, for another way-worn
  Child of Time in the grave must lie!
Closed one page of the solemn ledger,
  Head the next with another date:
" Hands, work on and, hearts, despair not!"
  Such be the motto of Eighty-Eight!

What if the skies are dark above us,
  Grim with terrors and big with doom?
God is great, and the souls that trust Him
  Rest secure in the deepest gloom.
Wildly over a world distracted
  The War-fiend sweeps with dread alarms,
But the man may smile at the storm who firmly
  Leans on the Everlasting Arms.

" There is nothing *beyond!* " says the sneering sophist,
  The poor blind bat who the light denies :
" There is nothing *beyond* for wretched mortals—
  No hope—no God in the silent skies ! "
Let him wrap his mantle of doubt around him
  And trust the lie that his lips proclaim,
But Love, we know, is the Lord of Heaven,
  Through the never-ending years the same !

And Love 'mid all the bewildering mazes
  Of the changeful æons and cycles new,
Still foreseeing, willing, directing,
  Holds in His hands the one sure clew,
Leads us on by a way we know not,
  Steadies our steps on the arduous road,
A shaft of light through the gloom to guide us
  To the pearly gates of his own abode !

THE PICTURE.

Beyond the smoke of the busy town
  And the dust of the whirring mills,
A spacious park and a stately house
  Stand on a spur of the hills ;
An old Elizabethan hall,
  With chequered lattice-work
And dark oak-panelled rooms, wherein
  All kinds of mysteries lurk ;
Reminding of that by-gone age
  Of happiness and health
In " Merrie England "—slain long since
  By dull material wealth !
And often there in the years gone by
  A pleasant hour I spent,
In the well-stocked library at ease,
  Book-worm to my heart's content !
Or pacing alone from room to room
  Gazed on the portraits rare,

Cavaliers of the olden time,
　　And ladies sweet and fair.
Here with a simper, there with a frown,
　　To mine their looks replied ;
I laughed to myself at the rudeness thus
　　Displayed on either side !
But one there was unfailingly
　　Among those pictures all,
Had power to stay my wandering steps
　　And silently recall.
" Marguerite at her Spinning Wheel "—
　　In the vestibule it hung :
Some unknown artist had painted it,
　　For whom fame had no tongue !
And yet poor Gretchen's pure young face,
　　And honest eyes serene,
Seemed to me always, as I gazed,
　　The sweetest I had seen,
Drew me for ever to the spot
　　And with a tranquil smile
Could, from my brow, of care and thought
　　The darkest cloud beguile.
And softly then, would I say to myself,

"O limner all unknown,
The power to lighten one human heart
  Is a great good gift to own,
And I thank thee much for thy 'Marguerite,'
  Though thanks can ne'er repay !
Oh, rarely on earth some get their dues,
  In a better world they may !"

THE DYING KING.

A King to-night lies in his chamber dying,
  Alone, neglected—he is old and worn!
Outside his courtiers, from his presence flying,
  Say with glad looks, "He may not see the morn!"

They cannot rest for restless expectation,
  They count the minutes with impatient sigh,
Tiptoe with eagerness and trepidation—
  Ah, will they do so when *they* come to die?

No more remembered their old master's kindness,
  His Royal favour, his majestic deeds,
Their eyes seem blinded with a stony blindness,
  And not one heart for him in pity bleeds!

Perish the old King! will that laboured breathing
    Drag on for ever? will the dull heart beat
As if for it not yet the blast were wreathing,
    Where the snow drifts, a chilly winding-sheet?

We want the young, the mirthful, and the pleasant,
    Ruddy of hue, blue-eyed, and golden-curled ;
Enough of gloom and drear face for the present,
    So the world wags, and we are of the world.

Cast off old friends and let them be forgotten!
    Old love, lie there!—our hearts are cold to thee—
Thy flowers are dead, thy garlands strewn and rotten,
    Nought hast thou left that gay and bright can be!

Lo ! a young monarch on the threshold meets us,
    Silent, emerging from the future's haze !
Unknown, untried, in dignity he greets us,
    With calm, inscrutable, mysterious gaze !

And through the night comes sound of bells in
        joyance,
    Ringing the promise of a nobler time,
All sombre cares, all sorrow and annoyance,
    Scattered before the music of their chime !

"Hail to the New Year!—Lordlings, bending lowly,
  Robe him in purple and with ermined cope!
What if yon dotard dieth slowly, slowly?—
  Crown the last-comer with his crown of hope!"

*   *   *   *   *   *   *   *

Old Year, Old Year, last year with hearts exulting
  We gave thee welcome and forgot the old,
And now—we spurn thee, sycophants insulting,
  And leave thee dying in the bitter cold!

TO OUR RULERS IN CHURCH AND STATE;

A VOICE THROUGH THE NIGHT.

January, 1892.

For God's sake strive to be true and tell the people
the truth,

Fronting the world with a fearless brow and with
fervour like that of your youth!

Why mumble and mutter, when asked to explain or
invited your views to expound,

With a nervous fumbling of fingers and a hang-dog
look on the ground?

You are Statesmen and leaders of men, so you say,
or leaders of thought, and you deem

That your wisdom indeed is transcendent, far beyond
what the populace dream,

And surely if God there be and the honour of Christ
is at stake,

Then to hold your tongues were a sin sometimes, and
your protest you should make.

But which of you, Sirs, in these perilous days when
the heart of the nation requires

Some comfort, some guidance, utters one word of its
real, deep desires?

You can flatter us, cringe to us, promise us much—
material boons and gifts!—

Pampering the brute of our being, while the soul
unheeded drifts ;

You can tell us that we are "as gods who know
both good and ill,"

That you only await our pleasure at once to work
our will ;

You can rouse our passions, inflame our greed, and
hound us on to crime,

But never a voice arraigns our sins or bids us pause
in time !

And now when sorrow afflicts us all and terrible
doubts assail,

And the torch of Hope lies quenched and dead, and
the lamp of Faith burns pale,

Why, if you believe as you say you believe in a life
beyond the grave,

Do you hesitate, fearing to tell men so? Is this to
be true and brave ?

Surely some of you far advanced in years, almost in
　　sight of its goal,

Must know at last, thro' the parting veil, the mystery
　　of man's soul,

Must be resting your hopes on a solid rock, earth's
　　stormy seas above,

And in God's infinite peace and rest have found
　　God's infinite love!

Poor miserables if you have not!—if before your gaze
　　alone

Ever a blackness of darkness hangs, and the path is
　　all unknown,

And after years of study and toil and unremitting
　　pains

No certainty has been reached at all, and no sure
　　hope remains!

Alas, for the reservations, the fears, the faltering
　　lips,

The carefully guarded accents—drear signs of Faith's
　　eclipse!—

The " whether there be a God or not, or beyond, a
　　heaven or hell

We do not know, and we may not know, and therefore
　　we cannot tell ! "

L

I am only a simple rhymster, unknown to the cliques
   and the sets,

Not one of the world's spoilt darlings, whom the
   world so soon forgets,

But this I know in my heart and feel is the lesson
   now for us all,

To own that God not man is great, and on His
   Name to call.

Do you doubt—can you question His power?—Gaze
   round the world and see

What signs and marvels and wonders in heaven and
   earth there be:

They cry that "the Lord God reigneth, and is King
   for evermore,

Bow down, rebellious hearts of men, and worship
   and adore!"

Yea, the days of retribution are crowding upon you
   at last,

And His arm is heavy with anger and His arrows
   strike you fast,

And the pride of the lofty is humbled, and the palace
   is dark with grief,

And the sound of mourning is in all lands, and there
   is no relief!

Not in human aid, not in human means!—yet if, with one long prayer,

A people knelt in the dust abased, and cast on Him its care,

If, pride abandoned and sins renounced, it sought His healing love,

Surely would fall the gracious dews of blessing from above.

And joy and health to its dwellings would soon return, and day

Drive darkness and death before it, and the plague have passed away,

And peace and gladness pervade all hearts in which He reigns as King,

Lord of the Universe, Lord of life, and Lover of everything!

"UNE FLEUR POUR REPONSE."

(From the French.)

" From this shore to distant regions, soon my vessel
    will be sailing,

And a long, long time I'll wander, ere again we two
    shall meet !

Will you give me now at parting, just one little pledge
    or token

That my heart some hope may cherish, though your
    love you give not, sweet?

Ah! farewell, Marie, I leave you! Woe is me! I
    sail to-morrow!

Oh, if you will not forget me, if your heart will feel
    some sorrow,

Give me from your hand, my darling, that fair rose-
    bud, I entreat !

" If that flower, that tender rosebud, were your gift to
    me at parting,

Ev'n in parting there would cheer me just one ray of
    happiness ;

And when far away from you, love, still my rosebud,
    fragile, faded,

Ever on my bosom resting, to my faithful heart I'd
　　press !

Ah ! farewell, Marie, I leave you !　Woe is me !　I sail
　　to-morrow !

Oh, if you will not regret me, if your heart will feel
　　some sorrow,

With the gift I crave, my darling, make me glad this
　　once and bless ! "

She, poor child, who 'neath his ardent gaze could only
　　blush and tremble,

Sad and pensive strove in silence from her heart on
　　God to call,

Whilst in accents low, reproachful, still he urged her,
　　still persisted ;—

" You are silent—you respond not !　Ah, you love me
　　not at all !

See, I leave you, broken-hearted !　Oh, farewell !　I
　　sail to-morrow ! "

And he turned as he were going, leaving her for aye
　　in sorrow ;

Then the flower, her only answer, from her hand Marie
　　let fall !

A LETTER OF CONDOLENCE.

(To the Rev. Bushby Thwackum, D.D., Head Master of
Whippingham Grammar School.)

My Reverend Friend,
      I much regret
To hear what trouble you have met
Where once with autocratic nod,
With birch, and cane, and pickled rod,
You wisely kept the boys at work,
And would not let the rascals shirk
The Latin Primer's noble pages
Stuffed with the lore of ancient sages !
Alas !—who ever heard the like ?—
Where you alone had power to strike
(And smartly for each sin or crime,
As I remember in my time,
Your arm, dear Doctor, used to fall !)
On strike, I'm told, your pupils all
Refuse your mandates to obey
And " terms " dictate to *you* to-day !

Truly, in topsy-turvy days
We live, and marvellous the ways
Of Nineteenth Century infants seem—
A wild, fantastic sort of dream ! "
They won't do this, they won't do that,
Contagion they have caught from Pat,
They scream, they kick, they howl, they shriek,
They will not let their parents speak,
And every Miss or Master Rowdy
Calls dad " a fool " and mother " dowdy ! "
As for authority or age,
These little tyrants in a rage
Have no respect for one or t'other—
One feels at times the lot to smother
Would be the safest thing to do
For England's sake and start anew,
For, seeing these are such a blunder,
What will *their* children be, I wonder ?
Mourning that such should cause annoy,
I sign myself

An Old " Old Boy."

"THE DOOR OF GOD."

A child on a couch by the window
  Gazing out to the west,
One bright October evening
  As the sun sank down to rest.

He watched the colours changing
  From ruby-red to gold,
From gray to dusky purple
  Along each surging fold,
Till a blaze of radiant glory
  Fell on his fair young brow—
One has never forgotten that moment,
  She sees that picture now !

Turning, he whispered to her,
  With a wistful sort of nod :—
" Tell me, is not that yonder
  The golden door of God ?

And will He not let me enter
  If I but humbly pray ?
I'm tired, so tired, dear mother,
  And care no more for play ! "
How could she answer her darling
  When tears were falling free,
In her heart a doom foreboding
  Which surely soon must be ?

* * * * * * * *

Alone on the couch by the window
  She sits with care opprest,
This mild October evening,
  Gazing out to the west.
Sorrow lies heavily on her ;
  She bows beneath the rod :
He has entered—but she waits still
  Outside "the door of God."

THE GOLDEN MONTH.

A sky where cloud and blue combine
To weave a canopy divine ;
A sun whose rays with genial heat
Slant mellowly, nor longer beat
With power intense on hill and vale ;
A gentle murmur in the gale,
That seems to pity every leaf
It wafts to earth, its hour so brief.
Across the lea, like thistle-down,
The silky gossamers are blown,
While dotted here and there gleam white
The fairy children of the night,
Who sudden rise in pastures green,
A miracle of growth unseen !
The river reaches, down below
The sloping uplands, tranquil glow,
Reflecting, like a burnished glass,
The fleecy clouds that o'er them pass,
And lazy cattle by the brink,

To lazy or to graze or drink.
And oh, to see, almost each hour,
What glorious gain, what golden dower
Brings Autumn to the stately trees,
The poet's, artist's, soul to please!
Ah, pleasant are the groves of June,
The nightingale's sweet plaintive tune,
The fragrance of the dark red rose
On which the summer dews repose,
But thou, September, calm and clear,
Hast all the riches of the year,
And from thy horn in ample store
Dost mellow wealth benignant pour.

"THE HOUSE ETERNAL."

Each man is building for himself,
  Ev'n while he sojourns here,
An everlasting dwelling-place
  By force of doom severe :
Inevitably, day by day,
  He must that structure rear.

The deep foundations of the house
  Are laid in childhood's hours,
Thence, stone by stone, the solid walls
  The pinnacles, and towers,
From ground to battlement complete,
  Youth furnishes and dowers.

Ceaseless, in manhood and in age,
  Some chamber or some hall
He, little recking that he works
  To destiny a thrall,
Fills with whatever goods of earth
  He values best of all.

Bright hopes which to his heart he hugs ;
  Grand dreams which crowd his brain ;
The words most frequent on his lips ;
  The deeds, with might and main
Commenced, completed—these therein
  Wait for his use again.

Pictured and panelled in each room,
  All acts which he has done,
All circumstances of his life
  Forgotten, past, and gone,
Faithfully imaged he shall have
  For aye to gaze upon.

All that in secret has been kept,
  Locked in his inmost breast,
Thoughts which he scarcely dared to think,
  But smothered and suppressed—
These shall confront him there, no more
  In gloom obscure to rest.

O solemn and abiding home,
  Man for himself uprears
In that far land which lies beyond

This vale of doubts and fears,
Wilt thou be cause of endless joy,
Or never-ceasing tears?

Ah! 'tis ourselves must blame ourselves
If torment, anguish, woe,
For ever and for ever fill
That house to which we go!—
Only who lives a God-like life
God's home of joy shall know.

TO THE LAST 'WOPSE" OF SUMMER

'Tis the last " wopse " of summer
  A-fooling around,
All his yellow companions
  Are dumb in the ground.
His flight is but feeble,
  He's down on his luck,
The apples all gathered,
  No syrup to suck !

Poor doited old beggar,
  Half-palsied your head,
To-night will be frosty,
  To-morrow you're dead !
Your life is a short one,
  Your summer soon goes,
But you won't have to shiver,
  Like me, in the snows !

So take my advice, sir,
    Crawl off to some hole,
And there before Vespers
    Be making your soul!
The flies buzz no longer,
    The swallows are gone,
Last "wopse" of the summer,
    Time's up, sir! move on!

LOST YOUTH.

(For Music.)

All Nature's choir is singing
    A carol blithe and gay,
The woodland copses ringing
    With welcome to the May.
Those feathered sprites no anguish
    Bids utter weary moan ;
Their joy can never languish—
    Remembrance is unknown !

The river reaches brightly
    Are flashing in the sun,
And o'er their mirror lightly
    The fleecy shadows run.
All flowers are gay together,
    The hawthorn in full bloom !
Earth gladdens at such weather,
    Released from winter gloom.

M

Life stirs around, above me,
 I hear it, and am sad,
None now, ah, none to love me,
 No friend to make me glad !
Long, long ago has faded
 What light was mine of yore—
A path, by sorrow shaded,
 I pace for evermore.

Gone, gone from me for ever
 The spring-time of my days,
And set those suns which never
 Relume their vanished rays.
Here in the woodland sadly,
 While skies above are bright,
And birds carolling gladly,
 I pause, and it is night !

TIRED.

I am weary of all this tumult, I am sick to death
   of this strife—

The Babel of cries and clamours perplexing modern life !

There is nothing in human knowledge solid or sure
   or true :

What know we more of the secret of things than
 . "the ape, our father," knew ?

Gold, Hypocrisy, Clap-trap, are the forces that sway
   mankind,

And the names of things and the things themselves
   at variance I find :

Monarchs,—mere ermined dummies, who have lost
   what power they had ;

Leaders—who follow the rabble to deeds however bad ;

Subjects—who will not listen to the Law's supreme
   command

Senates—where Treason marshals her vile, disloyal
   band ;

Churchmen—who have forgotten the good old-
   fashioned ways ;

Tories—who worship the Demos of these fantastic days |

In a medley of words unmeaning, the jargon by
    Science wrought,

We clothe our dearth of ideas and hide our lack of
    thought ;

Whilst ever in *salon* and college like a fountain
    gushes out

The chatter of hair-brained folly and semi-hysterical
    doubt.

'Tis the fashion to be Agnostic, and we listen while
    each wise fool

Parades his quips and his queries, like the prig of a
    Sunday School,

Scoffs at the Resurrection, and scarce knows what
    he means,

By his stale old sneers at " the herd of swine " and
    the fright of the Gadarenes !

Ah, frenzy of childish mortals, making so much ado

Because, after ages of learning, ye have mastered a
    page or two

Of the tiniest volume lying on the Infinite Author's
    shelves !

Now, God despised and forgotten, do ye deem ye are
    gods yourselves ?

Ay, prate of the constant ‘progress through all the
　　centuries made !

What mean you more, when you weigh your words,
　　than "the leaps and bounds" of Trade ?

And "the march of civilisation" is a phrase select
　　and nice

To cover the fact that the brute has grown, with the
　　years, refined in vice !

Or brag of the mighty wonders man's intellect has
　　done,

From the spark struck out of the flint-stone, to the
　　weighing of the sun !

But examine your boasting fully—does it aught of
　　Truth advance ?—

That accident first discovered, and *this* is a mere
　　" Perchance ! "

The facts which environ your being you comprehend
　　and see,

But who can explain the Ego ? .Or tell what Death
　　may be ?

Is it wisdom, to have discernment in the things we
　　handle and touch ?

Your gander, out on the common, knows, in his way,
　　as much !

Yet the chorus of approbation by every critic is sung,

For a venal Press from an age corrupt has naturally
sprung,

And in fatuous admiration through all the cliques
and the sets,

An Atheist's jibe or an Infidel's book the meed of
glory gets !

Low louting, we cringe before them, the Sages of
Science, the Wise ;

We hang on each word they utter ; the pearls of
their knowledge we prize !

From the prophets of evolution, puffed up by the
popular gale,

To the last weak, womanish scribbler, who has penned
some trashy tale !

Cry to them, worship them, praise them !—It is better
to pray to these

Than to fabulous God of the Christian to bend un-
willing knees !

Noble and grand, they never cherish a lie in their
breast,

Seeing the things which they wish to see and coolly
ignoring the rest !

Cry to them, worship them, praise them !—Send
"missioners" everywhere

That the people may be converted to the Gospel of
Despair !

Help forward a cause so precious by every means
you can,

Banish Faith from the visions of Childhood, drive
Hope from the heart of man !

Yet still from the poor old Bible, your scorn on its
dusty shelf,

Some wiser than you, will be learning the lesson "On
conquering Self,"

And a Voice from its pages stealing, to their inmost
souls will speak :—

" Lo ! Here in the Man of Sorrows is the Perfect
Man ye seek ! "

AT THE ACADEMY.

It was only a little picture
  In an unpretentious frame,
Just "skied" high up in a corner —
  I know not the artist's name!

A view of a little haven
  Far off on the wild Welsh shore—
A scene which I have not gazed on
These twenty years and more!

Brown hills, and a white-walled village
  Huddled away at their feet,
A church, a shop, and a tavern—
  You would hardly call them a street!

A valley, down which for ever
  A stream winds merrily,
And beyond, the heaving bosom
  Of the blue, unfathomed sea!

" Master-pieces," no doubt, were around me
  In gorgeous polychrome,
But I *loved* that little picture,
  For it spake to me of home.

THE TURN OF THE ROAD.

One night in a lonely valley, where the path was
rugged and rough,

I was plodding along but slowly, way-worn and weary
enough,

A high dark wall on my right hand, and sombre
pines on my left,

I seemed to be going forward, of the sense of sight
bereft,

Uncertain, in hesitation—'twas a path untried before,

And ever the darkness deepened around me more
and more.

At last, through a little cranny in the wall, a shaft of
light

Shot suddenly o'er the pathway, lit up the ebon
night,

And, the turn of the road before me, no distance now
to roam,

I knew that I soon would be standing in the cheerful
light of home!

   *   *   *   *   *   *   *   *

What is earth but the lonely valley? What life but
the path untrod,

Which, ever in darkness shrouded, we mortals all
must plod,

Weary and worn, and uncertain whither our footsteps
tend,

Yet wistful at last of a welcome when we have
reached the end ?

God's mansions are hidden from us, this wall of clay
between—

Perhaps it is best that we see not that far too dazzling
sheen !

Enough if, for present guidance, thus much the soul
divines

That here and there is a cranny through which His
goodness shines ;

Enough, though He tries our patience, and seems not
now to spare,

That the turn of the road is before us, and the heart's
true home is *there !*

LINES.

Oh to be eased of this burden,
 This uncongenial toil,
Worse than the manual labour
 Of the tiller of the soil !

Battling against a current
 Of ignorance and greed,
Blamed for each act of kindness,
 Cursed for each generous deed.

Oh to be free from the malice
 Of evil hearts and eyes,
And the tongues of fire that wither
 A man's fair fame with lies !

"THE YEAR IS DYING."

The harvest is past, the summer is ended,
    The redbreast 'plains in the berried thorn ;
The flowers, by weeping mists attended,
    To their grave, to their grave, in the dust arc borne,
And a wailing wind arises,
    And the world has grown forlorn.

One by one from the sycamore's branches,
    One by one from the chestnut tree,
Golden, russet, and bronzed are falling,
    The leaves, broad-green that used to be,
And the wailing wind arising,
    Shrills o'er the cold, grey sea.

No twitter now from the eaves at day-dawn,
    Tells that our summer friends are there ;
Only, at night, with a shudder, we hearken
    The grim owl presage a long despair,
And the wailing wind arises,
    And the fields are dull and bare.

Tired is Earth—'tis the way with the fickle !—
   Of her passionate lover, the bright-eyed sun ;
She turns from his glance to the gloomy wooing
   Of the wintry Night so dark and dun,
And the wailing wind arises,
   And the pleasant days are gone.

BUMBLEDOM.

'Twas a poor old widow, aged eighty-six,
   Who lived at Garden Square
On a shilling a week and a loaf of bread
   When the rent was paid for there.

" Parish allowance,"—" out-door relief "
   Is what 'tis called, you know,
The sort of kindness some Christian folk
   To other Christians show !

But a terrible crime this aged soul
   Was guilty of one day,
For she would not drive from her sheltering roof
   One poor lost girl away.

And the Bumbles of Bumbledom could not brook
   A case so sad to see,
Their pious souls were shocked to think
   Such wickedness should be !

So forth the edict went to dock
   This sinner of her dole ;
They were all so anxiously intent
   On saving—well—her soul !

There is One, I think, in another world
   Whose eyes survey this sphere,
And who judges things by a juster rule
   Than we too often here.

And perhaps He writes in His dreadful book,
   Which all must read ere long,
That this woman's "sin" was a glorious deed
   But the Bumbles' act a wrong !

THE CASE MISJUDGED.

Wandering on the shore one day
Strewn with boulders brown and gray,
Strips of seaweed, spiral shells,
Wherein the wild sea-music swells,
Pebbles, too, of varied size,
Coloured in unnumbered dyes,
Suddenly my stick laid bare
That which took my fancy there.

'Twas a rough, misshapen stone,
Lying by itself alone,
Buried in the sand almost
As desirous to be lost,
Shrinking—so a man will do,
Conscious of disgrace—from view!
Quoth a little lad thereat:—
"*I* should not care much for *that!*"

In my face with childish scorn,
As I held my prize forlorn,
And with patience cleansed away

Slimy seaweed, sand, and clay,
Gazed he—he was richer far!
Painted shells and gleaming spar
Rapture to his heart could bring!
What, to me, "that ugly thing?"

Who judge quickly judge but ill!
By the lapidary's skill
In my stone uncouth and strange
Has been wrought a wondrous change;
Polished, set in purest gold,
Laddie, now a gem behold
Fit on beauty's brow to gleam,
While your spar has ne'er a beam!

So in life the lesson learn
Not in foolish pride to turn
From whatever shows at sight
Vile, ill-favoured, void of light.
Even there a jewel lies,
Hid behind those sullen eyes,
That, by treatment kind and true,
Shall flash fair one day for you!

N

SOCRATES.

The hemlock works its will; a clay-cold hand
    Heavy as lead, hath seized my labouring heart;
Friends, who around my couch in sorrow stand,
    The hour is come, and we at last must part.

Yet not in horror from these earthly plains
    Shall I fare forth into the dark untried,
For I have confidence that there remains
    Being *beyond*, tho' Socrates hath died!

The last poor honours to my dust your care
    With tears will render, and, 'mid sighs and groans,
To gods infernal make the piteous prayer,
    That light the turf may lie upon my bones,

And many years of mourning for my sake
    Will ye endure, and infinite regret,
And bitter lamentations for me make
    " Whose day is done, whose sun for ever set '

Ah, say not so, belovéd friends! Believe
  (As I believe, and am assured shall be)
That *somewhere else*, whoso this dark world leave
  Find endless life and long tranquillity,

And there, in converse with the great of old—
  Just men and pious, innocent and wise—
Life's puzzling mysteries at last unfold,
  Seeing all Truth with clear, unclouded eyes!

Till then farewell!—Be virtuous, live for all
  That makes this dull world brighter, live as I
Have taught you!—But the solemn Parcæ call!
  I hear!—I come!—It is not hard to die!

JUST A MOMENT.

Just a moment, but a moment,
  One bright day not long ago,
In a garden where the roses,
  Fair white roses, bud and blow ;
She and I together wandered.
  Ah, the radiance of her face !
Ah, the beauty of the maiden
  Sweet and winning in her grace !

Just a moment, but one moment,
  Met our eyes without control ;
And I knew that she for ever
  Was the mistress of my soul.
    Ah, me ! Ah, me !
    That this should be !
But the chime of an old Italian song
  Heard somewhere, came to me—
" I plucked a rose, my dear one,
  And fell in love with thee."

Just a moment, but a moment,
  That bright day not long ago,
In that garden where the roses,
  Fair white roses, bud and blow,
She and I together wandered,
  And I dreamt I was in Heaven
While upon her dainty bosom
  Lay the rose that I had given.

Just a moment, but a moment,
  Met our eyes and told their tale,
But her face had lost its radiance,
  Cold and proud and lily-pale !
      Ah, me ! ah, me,
      So must it be !
The dirge of that old Italian song
  Comes sadly now to me—
" I plucked a rose, my dear one,
  And fell in love with thee ! "

IN THE CHURCH OF SAINT OSYTH, ESSEX.

In the quaint old Church at St. Osyth, I stood not
    long ago

(With its jumble of walls and arches, a curious place
    to show),

And I thought of the wretched medley of Christless
    sects and creeds

Which the world of to-day presents us, as year to
    year succeeds.

And then, as a painted window of somewhat gaudy hues

In the chancel rose before me, my thoughts began
    to muse

On the Past, and its wondrous stories of simple faith
    and love,

And the light on the brows of martyrs who passed
    to bliss above.

Here in the days of the Saxons, their idols cast away

When over the realm of England the Church of God
    held sway,

And all, in one fold gathered, adored the Crucified,

Nor, grieving the heart of Jesus, would wander far
    outside.

Osyth, the Mercian princess, a pure and pious maid,

Had built her a little convent half-hidden in a
glade,

And there, with a band of women who gave themselves to prayer,

Ever the sick and the needy and the wretched had
in care.

All loved the holy maiden, so gentle, kind, and
true,

The steps of the Heavenly Master who taught men to
pursue,

And thane, and ceorl, and franklin, seeing her blameless life,

Grew kindlier to each other and ceased from fraud
and strife.

But alas! one day o'er the waters a black fleet hove
in sight,

And there fell on the peaceful village wild panic and
affright,

"The Danes, the Danes are landing!" those cruel,
heathen hordes

Who spare not man or woman, but glut with blood
their swords.

In vain the Saxons faced them! the might of the
    foe o'ercame!

Hark to the shriek of the dying, the roar of the
 -    ruthless flame,

As cottage, and hall, and homestead, the dread
    destroyer takes,

And that scene of tranquil beauty a hideous ruin
    makes!

Haled by the savage Norsemen from forth the
    convent cell,

Like an angel taken captive by the demon hosts of
    hell,

I saw a pale, pure maiden dragged down to the wet
    sea sand,

'Mid blows and brutal insults from many a coward
    hand.

Bare was her snow-white bosom, her lovely arms
    were bare,

And the grasp of a lewd barbarian had seized her
    golden hair ;

But I saw her blue eyes lifted in faith serene on high,

And she passed to her doom unflinching, with neither
    moan nor sigh.

Only one little moment a voice came to my ear—

Above that ribald clamour it rose distinct and
clear :—

" Lord Jesu Christ, my Saviour, true God whom I
adore,

Now help me to confess Thee upon this blood-stained
shore !

" Into Thy hands my spirit right gladly I resign,

Thou gavest and Thou takest, dear Master, what is
Thine !

Yet hear the prayer of Thy handmaid, these men
their sin forgive,

And grant to their souls, repenting, through faith in
Thee to live !"

The flash of a blade descending ! Ah, swift and
sharp the stroke !

But the soul of that spotless lady from earth's dark
prison broke,

And soared on high to the glory God's blessed
children see,

For where Thou art, Lord Jesus, there shall Thy
servant be !

The years went by and the seasons with all their
changes vast,

But the prayer of the Mercian maiden not unregarded
passed ;

In His own good time the Master the paynim host
subdued,

And they bowed in meek submission before the Holy
Rood !

Then Asgard's halls deserted and darkness made to
cease,

And the days of error ended, set in the reign of
Peace ;

And the hammer of Thor was broken and Woden's
rule o'erthrown,

And the passionate hearts of the Vikings found rest
in Christ alone !

*   *   *   *   *   *   *   *

In the quaint old Church of St. Osyth, full of the
days gone by,

Recalling the martyr's story, hearing her dying cry,

Thus from my heart in the sorrow almost of deep
despair,

To the, throne of God in heaven arose one earnest
prayer :—

"Oh! that in this our England once more the Faith
   might be

Held by a Church united, one Church from sea to
   sea!

That our endless sects and parties might cease and
   be unknown,

And the passionate hearts of the people find rest in
   Christ alone!"

Ah! folly of fierce divisions and internecine strife,

When hungry souls are seeking in vain the bread of
   life!

Ah! Babel of mad confusion, and wild, conflicting
   cries,

None knowing and none discerning wherein true
   wisdom lies!

Yes, "the river of God" no longer flows through the
   land the same

As when from the Rock of Ages sparkling and pure
   it came!

Into strange channels diverted, lost amid rocks and
   sands,

Vainly men stretch towards it, athirst, their dying
   hands

And the sacred Truth's deposit, that store of Grace
    Divine,

That light by Heaven intended clear through all time
    to shine,

Reckless and inconsiderate, like children in their play,

We have taken the wealth God gave us and frittered
    it away !

A thousand roads to heaven, of modern date and new !

And the good old path Christ showed us is trodden
    but by few !

Each month, a fresh religion ! Each year, an altered
    creed !

Is the changeless God still changing, to suit men's
    whims indeed ?

So the faith of the many is feeble, and grievous harm
    is done,

And thousands of those called Christians no longer
    now are one,

And still, on our shores descending, harry us from
    without,

The pirate hosts of Error, the savage hordes of
    Doubt.

Parted, divided, scattered, to wolves an easier prey,

His lot for himself each choosing, the sheep of the
Shepherd stray,

In love with their own pet doctrines and plans to
save the soul,

Mere fragments of God's salvation, and never the
perfect whole !

Come back to the Church of your fathers !   Reseek
the Master's fold !

Renew in your hearts the fervour and the love men
had of old,

And pray for the martyr's spirit, for God unmoved
to stand,

Like the meek and gentle lady who died on yonder
strand !

"I AM NOT THE ROSE, BUT I LIVE NEXT DOOR."

A shy young man to a garden gate
  Timidly came one day,
Looked up the road and down the road
  In an undecided way.
" Myrtle Cottage," said he to himself;
  " I am sure that is the name,
But how may I know to which door to go?
  All look so much the same."

That shy young man to the knocker of brass,
  After many a pause from fear,
Contrived at length by exerted strength
  To make one hand draw near ;
And oh ! such a wretched little tap
  He tremblingly let fall !
Not even he could have hoped to see
  Response to such a call !

A bright little girl, with eyes so blue
  And such bewildering grace,
The door ope'd wide and saw outside
  That shy young man's red face !

" I beg—your pardon ! "—he blurted out,
    Blushing the more from fear,
" But—could—you—'er—tell—me—'er—if—well—
    If—Miss—Rose Smith—lives here ? "

That bright little girl, with eyes so blue
    And such bewildering grace,
Said nothing awhile, but with a smile
    Gazed in that young man's face.
Then with a toss of her golden curls,
    Which spake than words far more,
" I am not the Rose, Sir, goodness knows,
    But the Violet next door ! "

That shy young man, I know not why,
    Or what can take him there,
Day after day comes now that way
    With an expectant air ;
And poor Rose Smith is quite forgot
    And never asked for more—
That shy young man, with settled plan,
    Ne'er gets beyond " Next door ! "

MY LOVE, MY LOVE IS COMING.

They say that winter passes
   When March comes roaring in,
And wakes in leafless plant and tree
   The life that sleeps within.
I care not and I reck not,
   What change he brings the year;
My love, my love is coming,
   Already Spring is here.

The violet from the hedge-row
   Peeps timidly to see
If yet her friend the daisy
   Upon the trim lawn be.
O sweet, since you are coming,
   As sunlight seems it clear,
The violet will not peep in vain,
   The daisy must be here!

The birds in glade and covert
  Are merrily a-gate ;
Spring ne'er returns too early
  For them, or parts too late !
O sweet, since you are coming,
  My heart, no longer drear,
Breaks into song like yonder merle
  For joy its mate is near !

Wild winds of March, I hear you
  Come rushing, roaring in !
Wake, an ye please, in plants and trees
  The life that sleeps within !
I care not and I reck not
  What change ye bring the year !
My love, my love is coming,
  Already Spring is here.

o

THE BRITISH FARMER.

Nobody wants you, you poor old man,
Away to the workhouse as fast as you can,
The foreigners' corn, in price so low,
Will always into our markets flow,
And the urban populace find bread cheap,
When you no longer shall sow and reap!

True that the products, which even now
Follow the track of your ruined plough,
Larger and richer still by far
Than the products of manufactures are,
Yet placidly all your end will see
Provided "the cheap loaf" cheaper be!

Let farms lie tenantless, lands grow twitch,
Tangled each hedgerow, uncleared each ditch,
Let thistles, bine-weed, and docks be seen
In fallows once like a garden clean!—
"Feed," it is possible, to their mind
The donkeys of Free Trade there may find!

British ministers once took pride
In the prosperous state of the country-side,
But now their foreigner friends they court,
Giving them countenance, coin, support,
And nobody wants you, you poor old man,
So away to the workhouse as fast as you can!

Some day, when you moulder beneath the soil
Which you made so fertile by honest toil,
When a stalwart form and a strong right hand
Are sorely needed to guard our land,
They will long in vain for the yeomen stout
Whom the folly of England let die out!

TO SUMMER LINGERING.

Come, sweet Summer, come again,
  Queen of beauty, joy, and mirth ;
Bring the graces in thy train
  Down to earth !
Summer, we have waited for thee
  Many a long and darksome day,
Waited with an eager longing
  For the roses and the May,
For the pleasant smile thou wearest,
For the precious gifts thou bearest,
  Strewing thick with these thy flower-embroidered
    way !
See ! she comes ! she comes adown the sky,
  With glowing cheek and sparkling eye,
And tresses wildly to the zephyr flung,
  Her mantle of the emerald green,
Fairest of all the hues, 1 ween,
  In careless folds around her pearly shoulders
    hung !

On either side a frolic Love

Bends his bow and mischief schemes;

Ah! tender maidens soon shall prove

What dangers menace wheresoe'er each cruel
arrow gleams!

O Summer, Summer, welcome back

To these o'erclouded isles!

Drive from the blue its murky rack,

Till many-dimpled ocean smiles,

And all mad storms and icy tempests cease,

And plenty crowns the year with happiness and
peace!

IN BOYHOOD'S PRIME.

In boyhood's prime who thought of care,
　When all the birds would sing
From morn till eve, and never grieve
　Or 'plain for anything ?　·
And they were friends of mine, and friends
　Were butterfly and bee,
Their haunts I knew—far out of view
　They showed them all to me.
All day we babbled each to each,
　And oh, the tales they told
Of marvels rare that earth and air
　And pearly dew-drops hold !
Ah, golden hours of happiness
　And glorious summer sheen,
How sweet to me the memory
　Of your long vanished scene !

In boyhood's prime, all things aglow
　With love and life did seem,
And looking back, no dull cloud-rack
　Obscures its gay sunbeam,

Bright faces, laughing eyes, delights
   Of flowery vale and hill,
The warm west breeze, the whispering trees,
   The skylark's jocund trill,
The hum of insects in the air,
   The honey-suckle's scent,
The tinkling bell that told so well
   Where folded flocks were pent—
Such scenes, such thoughts, such sounds return,
   And must I yearn in vain
Just for one moment to go back
   To those fair days again ?

A careless lad who wandering,
   The noon and night between,
Down by the brook his way oft took
   To cull the sweet bog-bean,
And saw King Harry from his perch
   Above the reeds and willows,
Flash like a ray, and seize his prey
   'Mid Setchey's tiny billows :
Again, again, distinct and clear
   The sunny marge I see,

The blue forget-me-nots that grew
  There, only there, for me,
Or bare-legged, paddling up the stream
  I list the waters' flow,
That murmuring rill, that music, still
  Are in my heart, I know.

How often from the westering slope
  Where the green churchyard lies,
I viewed the crescent car of night
  In solemn state arise,
Awed by the splendours of the host
  That followed in her train,
Till wondrous thoughts and songs awoke
  In my young heart and brain !
Soon tired of books, from that broad scroll
  I could not turn aside,
Star-written by the hand of God,
  To humble earth's poor pride.
Ah, blessed hours of innocence,
  And holy, childlike awe,
Would that these eyes might now see Truth
  As plainly then they saw !

Hark ! 'tis the wailing autumn wind
    Across the stubbly fields !
And far and near, shrivelled and sere
    Its pride the woodland yields !
Yet, gaily o'er the furrowed breck
    His team the plowman steered,
And with a song both blithe and long
    Their plodding patience cheered !
Who dreaded *then* the falling leaf ?
    Or feared the wintry blast ?
Oh, boyhood's prime was that fair time
    When pulses bounded fast,
And sympathy knit heart to heart,
    And friendship man to man,
For high and low were then, you know,
    All brethren of one clan !

Kind Heaven, renew those golden hours
    In all their glorious sheen,
Just for one moment let me be
    That which I once have been,
Just for one moment *not* the man
    Whose mournful eyes to-day

Find little here to charm or cheer
    Life's pilgrim on his way !
Hush, fond lament !—repine not thou,
    Despair not thou, my soul !
In boyhood's prime, in manhood's time,
    God's tender, wise control
Hath been about thy path always,
    Nor aimless didst thou roam—
On to the end this constant Friend
    Trust thou to guide thee *home !*

THE PASSING OF WINTER.

O lurid skies of the even,
   O dark, portentous clouds,
Through which weird shapes are moving
   Like the dead in snow-white shrouds,
O gloom that gathers deeper
   As the wan sun disappears,
Of what to the world are ye symbols ?
   Lost hopes? or coming fears?

Or is it that winter, scowling
   Because death comes to him,
From the desolate North has summoned
   All that is drear and grim—
Storms in their rolling chariots
   And winds in wrath arrayed—
For the battle with Spring for Empire,
   For the strife which must be made?

Hark! clear through the sombre shadow
  O'er earth the tyrant flings,
A jubilant voice in the hedge-row
  Tells where the throstle sings,
Tells of the love which ever
  Survives all time and change,
Whilst along the path of the ages
  This orb of God shall range!

Pure in its simple beauty,
  Behold! the snow-drop gleams ;
And here and there in the garden
  Shoots up with golden beams,
As if the rays of the past June days
  Had taken root and grown,
And burst through the clods to cheer us—
  The crocus-flower full-blown!

And always, out in the woodland
  Where the dead leaves lie in heaps,
From some little nook turned sunward
  The blue of the violet peeps,

And shyly, with lips of fragrance,
  Seems saying in accents mild :—
"Stoop down and love me and kiss me.
  The year's wee darling child!"

O lurid skies of the even,
  O dark, portentous clouds,
I smile at the thoughts ye bring me
  Of the dead in snow-white shrouds,
For I know that the Life is waking
  Which has slept in its grave so long,
And the beautiful time is approaching
  Of gladness, growth, and song.

THE GOSSAMER:

OR THE THREAD OF THE VIRGIN.

(From the French.)

Poor little thread, that erst, a simple child
    And dreaming still,
I deemed abandoned by the Virgin mild
    To the wind's will.
Dear little thread, somewhere from her silk snood
    All rudely riven,
What cherub's breath now wafts, in idle mood,
    Thee far from Heaven?

Com'st thou from Bethlehem, that blest abode,
    Pale mist so rare,
Part of the frankincense that once to God
    The Magi bear?
Or, 'neath Nile palms, wast plucked by rough black
    thorn
    From mantle blue,
Wherein Heaven's Queen, poor mortal waif forlorn
    Hid God from view?

Com'st thou, as doves of old would come and bring,
    Couriers discreet,
A little hope beneath each snow-white wing
    Captives to greet?—
Thou dost recall calm eves of long ago
    When, veiled in white,
Damsels and youths, in solemn festal show,
    Marched through the night—

That innocent age, when all the soul was fain
    To love a flower,
And o'er the heart the organ's long refrain
    Had wondrous power;
When, with the dusk, towards one curtained spot
    A form would creep—
My glad-eyed mother's—bending o'er the cot
    To watch my sleep!

Adieu, frail film!—I love thee, onward borne!
    Yet go not thou
And wander where the wild rapacious thorn
    Thrusts forth its bough!
Tarry not here when on the high tower's rim
    Daylight has died,
But soar to God, for faithful loves with Him
    Alone abide.

A PEMBROKESHIRE "HEROINE.'

Shall I tell you of old Peggy Lewis
And the tale of her doings declare,
   A Pembrokeshire dame,
   Which is more to her shame,
For they used to be honest down there ?

She rented a wee bit of pasture
And had promised her landlord to pay
   The vicar his dues,
   And never refuse,
For " a bargain's a bargain " alway !

And because of that promise or bargain
Less rent to her landlord she paid,
   But to "stir up a breeze "
   For such reasons as these
Now-a-days is the Sectary's trade !

And a "heroine," Sirs, is a lady
Not given to keeping her word !
    Plainly put it in brief,
    A liar and thief,
Or a crazy old thing and absurd !

Not her's was the Tithe or the landlord's :
It belonged to the vicar alone,
    But this Pembrokeshire dame,
    Though you sing to her fame,
Took to grabbing what was not her own !

Why on earth in a matter of contract
Should Religion be dragged on the scene ?
    If you promised to pay
    Keep your promise, I say,
And honestly own what you mean !

But a hypocrite's part to be acting
Is unworthy Welsh woman or man !
    Parch Evans or Rees
    Of the chapel 'twill please,
But hide it from God if you can !

P

And you, Panegyrist of Peggy,
Your doggrel has brought you five pounds ;
   Disgraceful your gain
   On your hands leaves a stain,
And the doctrine you teach us astounds !

Wild words about " justice " you utter,
And laud this old trot to the skies,
   But you pograms know well,
   Of her wrongs as you tell,
The whole is a tissue of lies !

If your chapels commend us such morals
In regard to this matter, no doubt,
   Our account at the mill,
   Or the shopkeeper's bill,
Ere long 'twill be "pious " to scout !

And our " conscience " becoming so tender,
All our debts soon we'll leave in the lurch,
   Especially so,
   If it happens, you know,
That our creditors worship at Church !

BY NONA'S WELL.

Pembrokeshire, June 23rd, 1892.

Nona, Saint David's mother, she
Had well and shrine hard by the sea,
And on the slope above the bay
Still may you trace the two to-day,
The Holy well, where faith of old
Found mystic virtues manifold,
Whence glad of heart, the pilgrim passed,
Healed of his deadly plague at last,
(Or palsied limb, or sight obscured,
Or deafened ear, that instant cured)—
This still remains, yet sadly shorn
Of former pride ; its sides forlorn
With rusty lichens all bespread,
And a rank growth of weeds o'erhead.

But ruthless hands of time or man,
Or both combined, the worst they can
Have wrought against the lowly shrine

Which erst, O blissful saint, was thine!
Now fallen stone and crumbling wall
Too plainly tell its doom to all,
And silence on the place is laid
Where prayer to God was daily paid,
Save when at times the sea-mew's cry
Like some lost soul goes wailing by,
Or, from the strand, sounds fitfully
The dirge-like music of the sea.

And yet if sadness haunts the spot
And mourns o'er ruins, it is not
A sadness that may never cease,
But tender, melancholy peace
Comes with it to the troubled breast
Saying:—" Be comforted and rest!"
Dear land of Wales, my native land,
Stirred to the heart, again I stand
With sense and spirit drinking in
The weird, wild beauty of the scene—
That loveliness of sky and shore
Which thrilled me so in days of yore,

That broad expanse of waters blue,
Arched by a heaven as fair in hue,
Those bastions of the purple rock
Which brave the wintry tempest's shock,
Those heathered slopes and ferny vales,
Lying sequestered from all gales,
Along whose course fleet murmurous rills
Down from the everlasting hills—
Of things like these I never tire,
These lift my flagging spirit higher,
And dower my frame with more than wealth,
Renewing hope, restoring health !

THE MAGDALEN.

The world is beautiful now in spring,
   And bright is the deep blue sky,
But life to me is a loathsome thing,
   And I would that I might die!

Beautiful now is the hawthorn tree
   And the hedges white with May:
Down by the river and over the lea
   The daisies smile all day.

And far in the depths of the hazel-glade
   The nightingale sings to his love,
And beyond in the pine-woods' dusky shade
   You may hear the dreamy dove.

But I—— O God, I remember a day
   When I joyed in the pleasant spring,
Out in the meadow-lands wreathing the May,
   Ere life was a loathsome thing!

Now I turn from the world and weep,
  Gazing in anguish toward the sky—
By day no rest and by night no sleep!—
  Merciful Father, let me die!

There glides a vision before my eyes
  Of a cottage in a dell,
Whence the blue smoke coils to the bluer skies,
  My home before I fell!

And mother is knitting in her chair,
  And I am a little child,
With smooth white brow and nut-brown hair,
  And a spirit undefiled!

Thank God *she* sleeps in her quiet grave
  In the village churchyard now—
I have braved much, but I dare not brave
  Her sad, reproving brow!

Blind folly to leave those loving arms,
  That had shielded me for aye,
For a passion that only prized my charms,
  For an idle moment's play!

This morning I met him in the street,
  But he did not know this face,
And he spurned the groveller at his feet,
  With a smile of scornful grace!

Ah, where may rest for the ruined be?
  Or who will regard my call?
'Tis a curse or a blow for the likes of me,
  And the river—to end it all!

A HARVEST NIGHT.

The sun is down : a rosy hue
  Glows in the gray and golden west,
And o'er the broad, unclouded blue
  There comes a sense of perfect rest.

Clear to the view the prospect now,
  Valley and upland, where the sheaves
In adoration seem to bow
  In the warm light the day-god leaves.

Down hill the lumbering wains begin
  Homeward to bear the last huge load ;
Creeps from the river, white and thin,
  A mist. athwart the dusty road.

Across the stubble, whence the wheat
  Was carted with the early morn,
The weasel trots on nimble feet
  Towards the destined rabbit borne.

The partridge from the layer calls ;
   The hare slips through the well-worn gap ;
Bats flit around the old barn walls ;
   The owl, within awakes from nap,

And peering with her great round eyes,
   Through the wide wicket eastward sees
The great round lamp she loves arise
   With silvery sheen above the trees.

" Too-whoo-oo-oo ! "   In circling flight
   Adown the vale she speeds away !—
" Too-whoo-oo-oo ! "—A merry night
   To pass beneath that mellow ray !

Now, one by one the stars flash forth
   Their lesser lights round Dian's car ;
Wheel the twin Wains about the north,
   And westward Venus glints afar.

Falls heavy now on lawn and lea,
   The fay-beloved and sparkling dew
Fair weather both on land and sea,
   Foretelling, if old saws be true.

"LOVED AND LOST."

I stand apart in the ballroom—apart from the mazy
    throng,

Whilst the strains of that valse of Müller's float
    dreamily along,

And well does the music chime with " the thoughts
    that arise in me,"

As I ponder the past and the present, and the days
    that are to be.

The past, when I loved so dearly !—the present,
    when all is o'er,

And the light is lost for ever which lit my path
    before !

And now to face the future with the best heart that
    I can—

A task for a nerve of iron, and enough for any man !

Oh, lithe are the forms around me !—bright eyes
    that glow and glance,

And beauty made more luring by the soft, voluptuous
    dance—

But I heed them not, for in fancy my thought speeds
    far away

On the swell of the plaintive music the prim
musicians play.

And " Loved and Lost " is the burden of a dirge
within my brain,

Whose wailing phrases haunt me with a keen, re-
curring pain,

For I know how life henceforward must be despair's
sad thrall,

Ah ! surely it had been better not to have loved
at all !

So sang not one whose verses find more to praise
than blame ;

Did he ever love as I loved ? Was the loss he felt
the same ?

I know not, but I must wonder how a man should
not repine,

When his love was strong and trustful, and his loss
as great as mine.

ONE NIGHT IN JUNE.

AN OLD MAN'S TALE.

One night, when the stars were shining, and the
breeze and the woods were still,

And the moon in unclouded splendour, full-orbed,
clomb up the hill ;

We stroll'd along the pathway which leads to the
garden-side,

Gladys and I together, with love alone as guide.

The perfume of many roses stole up through the
stilly air—

I pluck'd a dewy blossom and twined it in her hair ;

And I said to it : "This my darling hath charms as
sweet as thine,

As sweet, but far less fading, and they all are mine,
are mine ! "

There passed o'er the path a shadow, and from the
distant sea,

A chilly wind came moaning across the level lea ;

Then a horror fell upon me, and I gaz'd with bated
breath,

For there, by the side of my darling, strode the
angel who is Death !

He strode by her side and beckon'd, and her colour
died away,

As before the night and its darkness I have seen the
rosy day :

In my arms I caught her and clasped her, and I
laughed, but it was not mirth,

For I saw—ah me !—departing, my last true light on
earth.

She died : friends gently laid her in the churchyard
of the glen,

And the years in long procession have pass'd away
since then ;

They have heaped their snows upon me, they have
bow'd me down with care,

They have blighted my hopes, but never have taught
me to despair.

For some night, when the stars are shining, and the
breeze and the woods are still,

And the moon in unclouded splendour, full-orbed,
climbs up the hill,

Along another pathway, which leads to a golden
door,

I shall pass, to be with my Gladys and love for
evermore.

THE CONSTANT KNIGHT.

A weary world is this indeed
  For wight that is forlorn,
For whom *les belles dames sans merci*
  Mete out contempt and scorn.
But foul or fair, I do not care,
  Let come what trial will !
I change not I, I can but sigh :—
  "Sweetheart, I love thee still !
    Gladness or rue, dear,
    Constant and true, dear,
  Sweetheart, I love thee, I love thee still !"

There are whose loyalty at best
  A fickle thing is seen ;
I cannot stoop so low to turn
  A traitor to my queen !
Nay, cold and cruel though she be,
  And ever treats me ill ;
I change not I, I can but sigh :—
  "Sweetheart, I love thee still !
    Gladness or rue, dear,
    Constant and true, dear,
  Sweetheart, I love thee, I love thee still !"

Though to my prayers she pays no heed,
  Or answers with disdain,
Or with the flash of angered eyes
  Adds torment to my pain ;
Though never smile or gentle touch
  Balm on my wound distil ;
I change not I, I can but sigh :—
  " Sweetheart, I love thee still !
      Gladness or rue, dear,
      Constant and true, dear,
  Sweetheart, I love thee, I love thee still ! "

Let life be dark because on me
  No gentle sunshine falls ;
No rapture on the battle-field,
  No joy in palace halls !
'Tis better as it is, ev'n though
  Sad tears mine eyelids fill !
I change not I, I can but sigh :—
  " Sweetheart, I love thee still !
      Gladness or rue, dear,
      Constant and true, dear,
  Sweetheart, I love thee, I love thee still ! "

"AN ALIEN CHURCH!"

" False are the tongues that say the words,
  Untrue the statement penned ! "
Such is the record of the hills,
  The message that they send.
Go, search the land from north to south,
  From Ramsey to Lisvane ;
The writing on the wall of Time
  Unaltered will remain,
Stamped on the hamlet and the town
  Inseparably part
Of every Welshman's daily life
  In farm and mine and mart !
Love for your native land you boast
  Its language, story, fame—
The silent witness these afford,
  Unheeding to your shame.
Your ancient chieftains' homes are dust
  Your ancient Bards are dead,

Q

But still the venerable Church
   Uplifts her stately head,
No ruin desolate, forlorn,
   But claiming to this hour
The presence of her God—the might
   Of superhuman power !
A thousand old familiar spots,
   Her living force proclaim ;
Founded upon the Rock of Truth,
   Eternally the same.
A thousand old familiar words,
   Tell how of old the light
Was kindled by the priests of God
   In heathendom's dark night.
And He, we trust, Who gave that light,
   Shall cause it still to burn,
Till to their mother's longing arms
   Her wandering sons return.
Llandaff, Llangollen, and Llanrwst—
   Say what such titles mean—
They cry that there your "alien Church"
   For centuries has been.
They point to what your fathers were

In noble days gone by,
Content in *one* true Faith to live,
  And in that Faith to die.
Then, gathered in one hallowed house,
  God's home, the house of prayer
Christ's people were one family,
  Nor sect nor faction there,
Then, kneeling at one sacred feast,
  They sought one dying Lord,
And broke the Bread and drank the Wine
  And worshipped and adored,
Bound to each other by the cords
  Of brotherhood and love,
They served the Master here on earth
  And passed to rest above.
But where were then the heresies,
  Of which ye vaunt in pride,
Out from whose cold and barren creed
  All fire of faith has died ?
Where, too, your chapels then (in which
  Alone is Truth, ye say),
Those fungus growths of ignorance,
  Corrupted in a day ?

Those " blissful " shrines that harbour *now*
   Hypocrisy and greed,
Or murderous thoughts which make afresh
   The wounds of Christ to bleed?
Ah ! " Christianities " become
   Mere shadows of a name—
The shoddy robes which cannot hide
   The underlying shame—
Ah, solemn frauds that pit yourselves
   Against the Rock Divine,
" The city of our God " shall stand,
   Her steadfast beacon shine,
When your poor *ignes fatui*
   Have ceased to lead astray,
And slanderous tongues and lying lips
   For ever passed away.

THEIR ANSWERS.

I.

Old man, with white hairs sparse
 Upon thy withered brow,
 Here on this windy shore
  What seekest thou?
Thy lean hand grasps a fragile little shell,
 'Tis tenantless and bare,
 No living beauty there!
What secret from that cenotaph would'st thou by
 force compel?

"I seek for Life," he cried,
 "And I have never rest,
 Here on this barren shore
  In endless quest!
Rocks, seas, and sands, earth's treasures, I ransack,
 Yet cannot search it out,
 For still the subtle doubt,
Like the cool lymph from straining lips of
 Tantalus, flies back!"

2.

Poet, with ardent gaze
    Turned to the starry skies,
What of the worlds unknown
    Dost thou surmise?
Strewn with the brilliant fancies of thy soul,
    Show not those orbs of light,
    Now doubly pure and bright,
Realms of eternal rest, domains in sweet, young
    Love's control?

    " Love?" with a groan, he cried,
      " We seek him everywhere,
    Lone on this dreary shore
      In dark despair!
The stars but mock us, earth has ne'er a smile!
    Alas, poor mortal race!
    The same dull round we pace,
Lured to our doom from youth to age by false
    Hope's treacherous guile!

3.

Child, with the dove-like eyes,
    What visions fill thy mind,
Thus by the fountain's marge
    In thought reclined?

Above thee, soaring in the sunlit deep,

  The sky-lark mounts for aye,

  Singing her soul away,

Climbing those dazzling stairs that erst God's
Prince beheld in sleep!

  " Ah," with a rush of tears,

   Turning, he made reply,

  " But now, methought, I learnt

  The reason why

The lark went soaring ever, singing too!

  Why came you here, to break

  Such pleasant dreams? Awake,

I see no more those glorious things!—All gone,
because of *you!* "

4.

  Maiden, with 'raptured face,

   Whose fingers strike the keys

  Of the great organ till

  Their harmonies

Thrill thro' our souls and ravish with delight,

  Ah, say what seest thou more

  Than on this barren shore

Comes to us men of ruder mould and dowered
with duller sight!

" I see the Light that streams
  From God enthroned afar,
Beyond the brightest sun,
  The fairest star !
I hear the music of the blest above !
  Oh, hush ! what strains there be
Upon that crystal sea—
The song of souls redeemed, the praise of
  Everlasting Love ! "

HOW PRIAM PLEADED WITH ACHILLES FOR THE DEAD BODY OF HECTOR.

" What dost thou here ? " the hero cried,
   " What wouldst, old man, with me,
Clasping my knees with suppliant hands,
   Weeping so bitterly ?
Art thou not Priam, god-like chief
   Of Troy's embattled town,
Father of princes, lord of lands,
   Monarch of high renown ?
How cam'st thou here amid the Greeks,
   Thy foemen every one ?
What seek'st thou trembling at the hands
   Of him who slew thy son ? "

Sternly he spake, yet pitying
   Old Priam's bitter woe,
And all men marvelled, seeing there
   That grey head bowed so low.

" God-aided to thy tent I came,"
   He answered and replied ;
" The wingèd Messenger of Zeus
   Sped forth to be my guide.

He brought me from broad-streeted Troy
   Across the darkling plain ;
He stilled my clattering chariot-wheels,
   And hushed the lumbering wain :

So fared I on and passed unharmed
   All dangers of the way,
And here, large ransom in my hands,
   I kneel, a boon to pray.

What words may wretched Priam use
   When words are all too weak ?—
Oh, let these sighs and groans and tears
   More powerfully speak !

Bethink thee now "—and tears ran down
   His furrowed cheeks in streams—
" What conduct, dread Achilles, best
   The truly brave beseems ?

Thou hast a father !—his grey hairs
   Shall bid thee rev'rence mine !
What sorrow fills my broken heart

Thou might'st by his divine,
Should aught to thee untoward hap,
  By stern decree of Doom,
Or mournful tidings of thy death
  To aged Peleus come !
How sad, forsaken, then his plight,
  Reft of his only son,
Lone in the world, protectorless,
  And utterly undone !
Yet he, rejoicing, knows that thou
  Still seest the light of day,
And hopes each dawn may bring thee safe
  Home o'er the white sea-spray.
Fifty in number, stalwart youths,
  His sons could Priam call,
And aye was Hector first and best,
  The noblest of them all !
But now to me, their luckless sire,
  Meseems, no sons remain
Of all that brave and comely band,
  Requiring *one* in vain,
Hector, my pride, my star, my joy,
  The bulwark of my throne,

Sole stay of Troy and Priam's house,
     In whom I lived alone !
Slain by thy hand, Achilles, he
     Lies cold in death indeed !—
Yet kneel I even at thy feet
     For his release to plead !
Hear thou my prayer!—respect the gods!—
     The priceless ransom take !—
Look pitying on a father's grief,
     Yea, for thy father's sake !
For surely in this so wide a world
     Was never wight before,
'Mid all the myriad tribes of men,
     Woe such as Priam's bore ;
And never of old was suppliant known
     Dared do what I have done,
Stooping to kiss the blood-stained hand
     Of him who slew my son !"

He ceased, and pity filled the heart
     Of each man there that heard,
And stern Achilles, greatly moved,
     With pity, too, was stirred.

The grey hairs of his father seemed
    To rise before his view ;
With one broad hand his eyes he veiled,
    That tears did now bedew,
The other to the suppliant stretched
    Who grovelled at his feet,
Saying : " Arise, such posture vile
    In old age is not meet ! "
Sore wept they then ; the one in grief
    For Hector lost and dead ;
The other, thinking of his sire
    And how Patroclus bled !
Gently did great Achilles raise
    Old Priam up, and say
Words comforting, his bitter pain
    To solace and allay ;
Declaring also how to him
    The will of Zeus was known,
For sea-born Thetis to her son
    Heaven's high behests had shown.
" I give thee back thy son," he said,
    His body I restore,
The priceless ransom I accept,

What can Achilles more ?
But oh, Patroclus, comrade mine,
   In realms of darkness laid,
Forgive if I do aught amiss
   Who thus thy slayer aid !
No paltry price shall I receive
   To grant a father's prayer,
And thou, dear friend, O best beloved,
   Shalt have thy fitting share ! "

*   *   *   *   *   *   *   *

Thus Priam fared in days of old,
   Thus was his errand done,
Thus heavenly pity stirred the heart
   Of Peleus' god-like son !
And if no mark on earth remain
   To tell of Ilion's fall,
Green grow the grass where warriors fought,
   Oblivion shroud them all,
Yet lives the Blind Bard's wondrous song
   A father's love to show,
And tell, from savage eyes of hate,
   How tender tears could flow !

Ah ! would that hearts might oftener melt
   When misery's tale is told,
And kindled be the flames of love
   In breasts now stern and cold ;
For so the whole wide world would move
   Upon a nobler plan,
And Wrong die out, and Right prevail,
   And man be dear to man !

TO MISS ALICE FOX. OF TENDRING.

On her completing her 100th year, March 4th, 1892.

Born in the turbulent, dark days
Of Revolution, when the thrones and faiths
Of Europe tottered, and alone intact,
The heart of England, like her hearts of oak
Sound to the core, could fearless front the world,
And threat'ning dangers did but courage add
To souls courageous with high thoughts inspired,
Days when that brave old admiral was born
Whom but a month ago they laid to rest
In the calm churchyard 'neath the eye of God,
His last great battle fought, to thee I send,
Remembered in the past, a kindly line
Of salutation, praying that the life
Guided so long in quiet, peaceful paths,
And blessed so freely with our Father's love,
On to the end as tranquilly may pass.
A hundred years!—What mem'ries crowd thy brain,
What faces haunt thy dreams and call thee back

To days of childhood when thy feet ran light
O'er croft and wold, and in the sweet spring time
Were blossoms on the orchard apple-trees
And blossoms on thy cheeks, and mirth and health
Laughed on thy lips and sparkled in thine eyes !
A hundred years !—What changes thou hast seen,
What pleasures proved, what sorrows felt and shared!
Changes around, in families and homes,
Changes in nature, changes in the world,
Old landmarks vanished, dear familiar trees,
Hedge-rows and gardens, pathways through the fields,
The village green, the rustic bridge that spanned
The noisy runnel, altered all or gone !
A hundred years !—Look back and ponder o'er
The sad vicissitudes of cruel Time !
How many hands have grasped those wrinkled hands
(Not wrinkled once) in welcome and good bye !
How many eyes, long since for ever closed,
Gazed into thine with sympathy and love !
What voices, once familiar, sound no more
In gentle or in friendly accents now—
Like his, that kind good man, whom I recall,
For forty years your pastor and your guide,

R

Who waits to greet you on the farther shore!
True, all are gone, the loved ones of those days
And days that followed, yet if much be lost
Much still remains!—Hark, still the sweet church bells
Are ringing, and their music, as of old,
Comes to the heart and tells thee "God is love!"
Still, still the old Faith lives, for all the doubts,
For all the changes of this weary world!
Still, still its comforts fail not!—Still the hope
Of re-uniting in a fairer home
Burns ever brighter, and not less for thee
Abides that promise, fixed and sure, of Him,
Who is the Resurrection and the Life,
"Because I live, ye shall live also"—*here*
In this dark world, supported by the love
That loves and dies not, cheered by patient hope,
And with the eye of faith the things unseen
Beholding—*there*, in pastures of the blest,
Age lost in endless immortality,
Changed this vile body, ev'ry power restored
For ever and for ever with the Lord!

THE OLD FARM HOUSE.

I remember once, as I wandered thro' a valley in wild
    North Wales,

I came on a spot at even, shut in from the Western
    gales,

And there by an alder thicket was a farm house old
    and grey,

A lonely, moss-grown structure, untenanted many a
    day.

The door with its falling side-posts and rusty hinge
    and latch,

The shattered panes of the windows, the roof with
    its rotten thatch,

Gave to the house an aspect no language could
    explain—

Methought, I had one day seen it, in a poor dumb
    beast in pain !

Half-choked in a tangle of nettles, one drooping
    blush-rose bloom

In the desolate garden struggled the night-air to
    perfume,

With a motion apologetic as if it said : " Forgive !—

I could wish you a warmer welcome—but you see the
    way I live ! "

Opening the door, I entered and stood in a dreary
hall,

Cobwebs and dust on the ceiling, green slime along
each wall,

And here on his back a beetle sprawled, taken un-
awares,

And there, in stolid amazement, a toad at the foot of
the stairs !

I passed through rooms deserted, the blackened
hearths all bare,

No sign of the cosy kettle that erst sang blithely
there,

No voices of little children gay-prattling as of yore,

Only the dismal echo my steps drew from the floor !

The silence became oppressive, the loneliness a
dread,

And weird were the fancies thronging that moment
in my head,

For the people, with whom I peopled those chambers
drear and dim,

Had eyes worn wild with sorrow, and faces gaunt
and grim !

Mounting the steep, oak staircase, a room I found on
    the right,

Whose solitary lattice gave only a feeble light,

And there on the sill, its pages mouldering into
    decay,

Someone had left a Bible, before he passed away.

I stooped—for the book was open, a mark set at the
    place—

And at last in the dusky glimmer, I read these words
    of grace,

Full of a blessed promise surely not yet to
    cease—

" I will fill this house with glory, and in this place
    give peace ! "

In through the broken lattice there burst a sudden
    gleam,

Illuming the page before me, casting a silvery
    beam,

On wall and flooring and rafter, in that forsaken
    room—

The mild, soft rays of the moonlight made beautiful
    the gloom !

Lo! the sad strange thoughts within me all suddenly
    had fled,

And the mournful shapes I had fancied grew angel-
    eyed instead,

Smiling upon me sweetly, while voices far and near

Like Æolian music murmured : "Glory and peace are
    here!"

*   *   *   *   *   *   *   *   *

It is long since I left the ruin in that sequestered
    spot,

Perhaps it has now a tenant, or, likelier far, has not,

Yet often as I remember how I found the Bible
    there,

A quaint thought rises in me which takes the form
    of a prayer!

In this house which I inhabit, this wonderful house of
    clay,

From which all grace and vigour soon, soon, must
    pass away,

God grant in thy chamber, Mem'ry, at the close of
    my earthly strife

I find if it be but a fragment of the precious Word
    of Life!

THE THREE SISTERS

A LEGEND.

Once in some forgotten island.
  So an ancient writer saith,
Lived three gentle orphan sisters,
  Honour, Loyalty, and Faith.

Daughters of a king, and noble,
  Fair their forms to look upon,
Fresh as rosebuds in the morning,
  Ere the early dew is gone.

And there spread among the people
  Such a fame about the three,
That they came from far off countries
  But one glimpse of them to see.

And there went a saying also
  Up and down the wondering land,
That so long as these were living
  Throne and commonwealth should stand !

Dwelt they in a little cottage
  Nestling in a quiet glen,
Doing good to all around them,
  Shunning vain applause of men.

Long in peace they lived together
　　Cherished and revered by all,
Till there chanced a time of trouble
　　To that island did befall.

Wicked men and evil counsels
　　Were prevailing in the state,
And to crime they urged the people,
　　Crime too dreadful to relate!

" Seize," said they, "those orphan sisters,
　　They are harlots and should die!
Give their cottage to our handmaids,
　　Treason, Blasphemy and Lie!"

And the people seized with madness
　　As the people are at times,
Listened to the evil counsels
　　Of the men who practised crimes.

Honour to a land transported
　　Lying some way from their shores,
Left they to be gored and murdered
　　By a savage herd of boars.

Loyalty they slowly poisoned
　Mocking her with heartless jibe,
With the drugs some Irish doctors
　Even now, I hear, prescribe.

Faith they handed to a demon,
　Who assuming mortal shape,
At that time was teaching people
　God was nothing but an ape.

　Laying strict injunctions on him
(Not that these were needed much)
　Evermore to bruise and beat her
And defile her with his touch.

But men say, that when the monster
　With a frown of hate drew near,
Faith arose and went to meet him
　Calmly smiling, free from fear.

Smote him not with brand or buffet
　But with one look from her eyes:
At her feet as lightning-stricken
　Lo! a blackened corse he lies!

Came a car with fiery horses
    By a dazzling seraph driven.
Caught up Faith and bore her deathless
    To the throne of God in Heaven.

Then the people stood astonished
    Gazing at that awful sight,
And their souls the madness quitted,
    And they knew their wretched plight.

Turned they then with shrieks of anger
    And despair's impassioned cry,
Caught those wicked ones and slew them
    With their handmaids cowering by.

Cursed the folly which had brought them
    To so vile and dark a deed,
As to cause the blessed maidens
    From their midst to pass and bleed !

" But no more," that ancient writer
    Adds, " in that unhappy land,
Those fair lives for ever vanished,
    Throne and commonwealth might stand."

OUTSIDE.

I.

Hard by the old Cathedral, facing its southern wall,

On the slope of the daisied graveyard, shut in by railings tall,

Is a slab with a Latin inscription, and calm in sleep below,

My mother and little sister who died long years ago.

And there one April morning, when the grass grew fresh and green,

And not one fleece over all the blue of heaven's broad mead was seen,

Outside those iron railings I stood and wept and prayed,

For oft, tho' the sun be shining, man's heart is sore dismayed !

"O mother," I cried in anguish, "listen, I pray, to me,

The babe that you left, in manhood toss'd on life's stormy sea,

Here, to your grave, has drifted, and yearns for peace and rest—

Let me lay my head, dear mother, down on your gentle breast ! "

There in my passionate sorrow and agony of thought,

To touch the soil that concealed her with hands
outstretched I sought,

But the iron rails forbade it, and grimly interposed,

And meseemed that their icy fingers around my
heart had closed.

      *   *   *   *   *   *   *   *

Hark ! 'Twas a strain of music stole softly on my
ear,

Thro' the old Cathedral arches an anthem sweet and
clear,

And the choir-boys' notes seraphic fell on my heart
like balm,

And hushed was the storm of passion into a holy
calm !—

"Oh ! rest in the Lord, committing thy way unto
His care !

Wait patiently upon Him and He will answer prayer,

Yea, God shall cause all sorrow and sighs and tears
to cease,

And at even-tide to the weary soul there shall be
light and peace ! "

II.

Outside the iron railings in this dark world we
stand,

Where seems no heart to pity, no kind, uplifting
hand ;

But we see not *all* before us, we know not yet *the
right,*

Nor mark at our side for ever Christ walking thro'
the night.

Nay, oft in our desolation a cry goes forth to Him,

Like the cry of despair that pagans shriek at idol-
monsters grim,

And we deem that He recks not, cares not, nor
pities any one—

While the bars that keep us from Him are the sins
that we have done !

With passionate eager longing and agony of mind,

With hands outstretched we seek Him, if haply we
may find,

With passionate eager longing for pardon, peace and
rest,

We would lay us down, contented, upon His gentle
breast.

And the prayer of hearts bewailing goes up to God
    above :

" Look down on Thy children drifting far from their
    Father's love,

Break Thou the iron railings of miserable fate,

Hush Thou the voice within us that cries ' Too late !
    Too late ! ' "

* * * * * * * *

Hark to the solemn music ! It swells, an anthem
    clear

Thro' the old Cathedral arches of Nature far and
    near !

In the forest-glade—on the mountain—by the deep,
    resounding sea—

The voices of God are singing, despairing Man, to
    thee :

" Oh ! rest in the Lord, committing thy way unto
    His care !

Wait patiently upon Him and He will answer prayer,

Yea, God shall cause all sorrow and sighs and tears
    to cease,

And at even-tide to the weary soul there shall be
    light and peace ! "

AN OLD TRUE-BLUE
TO A CONSERVATIVE FRIEND.

You ask me why so seldom now
My "caustic rhymes" in print appear,
And hint—a charge I'll not allow—
I lazier grow from year to year.
If you must have my reasons out,
Little I find to write about.

What is there in this languid age
To stir the blood or fire the soul?
Our climate chills poetic rage,
And social laws our tongues control;
Fervour, enthusiastic zeal
Tabooed—'tis *such* bad form to *feel!*

Truth?—Look in vain for her plain face
In all this false, deceptive throng!
She's out of date, or in disgrace—
A virtue now not worth a song.
Banished once more, the truth to tell,
To the dark depths of her old well!

You say my *bête noir*, Gladstone, still
Pursues his old destructive work,
Hounding the Irish on to ill
As erst the Russ against the Turk.
What audience applauds his tricks?
Rogues, murderers, and lunatics!

"Our leaders?"—If they would but lead,
Not follow, as the vogue has been
The last six years, the track of greed,
Where statesmen once were never seen!
Your humbug Tory-Democrat
Perpetual mischief now is at!

"Wants of the day!"—That means, dilute
Eternal verities, to please
The fancy of the anarch brute,
The whims of those who prey and seize,
Attentive to the wild beast's cry,
And prompt the knave to satisfy!

For bread the poor cry out, not stones;
For work the working classes call;
The Legislature's "Only Jones"

Is equal to occasions all :
Comes, famished mouths to stop and fill,
A brand-new Plunder-Some-One Bill!

So much we love the Faith, we grudge
Each penny which to God we give !
" The rights of property ? "—all fudge !
Dishonest rogues at least must live ;
And so in Wales, in England, too,
Deprive God's servant of his due !

Drink at your Party dinners, friend,
The good old toast of " Church and Queen ; "
The monarch's power is at an end ;
Soon will the Church no more be seen !
And only this your pledge denotes,
That still on both depend some votes !

" Convictions—principles," good sir ?—
You prate of things long passed away !
The names survive, but cannot stir,
One politician's heart to-day !
" Opinions " now alone we see,
Pray, where to-morrow will *they* be ?

s

"We'll save the Empire!"—so you cry—
Heaven grant it!—but don't be too sure
Yours is the only way to try,
Or that your plans will prove secure!
Next General Election may
Surprise you rather, some folks say.*

Nay, though you save it in one sense,
And stop the spread of Treason's tide,
Are there not dangers as immense
May rush in on the other side?
Whilst foes external you repel,
Are *those internal* faced as well?

Here, here in England's heart, at rest,
Yet not at rest, wild passions lie
Which some day—*not* when you think best!—
Shall shake the earth and storm the sky!
An adversary hard to cope,
The multitude that has no hope!

---

* It did do so in 1892.

THE PRE-ADAMITE PECTUNCULUS.

A shell they found at Walton-on-the-Naze,
Carved with quaint carvings, "mystic, wonderful."
A pair of eyes thereon were two round holes,
A downward scratch did represent a nose,
And one transverse, the sweet, persuasive mouth.
Deep buried in the loose, primeval crag
" For centuries and for æons" had it lain
This small Pectunculus, this tiny shell,
A silent witness to the solemn past,
And all the hoar antiquity of Man.

Received with rev'rence, handled with much awe,
Studied, examined, every groove explored
Cut by the flint-knife of that artist old,
The scientists exulted o'er that shell,
And many a letter to the journals penned,
Fraught with the wisdom that " explaineth all,"
Expounding theories infallible :
'' Here, here was proof, irrefragable proof,
If proof were needed, that the race of man

Far back upon the dusky stream of Time
(Long, long before those poor, misleading myths
In *Genesis* recorded, *Chapter I.*)
Had ta'en their course and lived their perilous lives,
Dwelling in caverns, miserably clad,
Worse armed against those old invet'rate foes
The bear, the python, and the grisly wolf!
Yet dull and brutish if the many were,
A little nobler than the Ape, their sire,
Trace here th' enlightened few! For certainly
In relics such as this most precious shell,
Cleared of all clouds the eye of wisdom sees
Faint adumbrations of the Coming Man,
The Man as now we know him, glorious, great,
Wise, sage, sagacious, in all arts supreme,
All sciences consummate, Man that needs
No power beyond him as of fabulous god,
Christian or Pagan, Man that is alone
In all things self-sufficing, self-complete,
Master of Nature, lord of all the worlds!"

So in an old museum's dim glass case,
With other "finds" as marvellous and queer,

They placed, these *savants*, their Pectunculus,
And for some months " the scientific world "
Discussed, disputed, wrangled, raged thereon.
In sooth a controversy was stirred up
(The fires of which not yet have been allayed
But still burn fiercely in the big reviews)
'Twixt two geologists, both men of mark,
Whether the features carven on that shell
Were those of Simian man or Simian maid,
And vast the quantity of ink they slang.

Now, as it chanced, to that museum came
One day a father with his little son,
Who pausing by the glass case dusty, dim,
All suddenly, "O father" cried the lad,
" Look at this very funny little shell ! —
I could have cut a face as good as that ! "
The father turned, amused at what amused
His little one, and as he looked a smile
Of keen enjoyment o'er his features stole,
A smile, it seemed, of recognition too !
Then, drawing near more nicely to discern
The parchment legend that beside the shell

Set forth its history, and name and date,

A fit of merry laughter shook his frame.

Then, while the lad astonished at him gazed :

" My boy," said he, " your father years ago

Carved with his knife upon the Walton sands,

The lineaments you scoff at in that shell !

The time, the place come back to mem'ry's view

As sharply and distinctly as it were

But yesterday !—and—oh, the folly of it !—

The rare absurdity !—I, plain John Smith,

Grocer and draper, North Street, Kentish Town,

Am the Pre-Adamite Anthromorph,

The carver of this same Pectunculus,

The Flint Jack of those far, primeval days,

The savage Troglodyte, the Missing Link ! "

IN RAINY ESSEX.

"Oh! for one hour of the Sunny South,
    One glimpse of a sky serene,
Afar from the dull and leaden gloom
    Which forms an English scene!

Oh! for one breath of a purer air,
    Than our flagging spirits know.
In that purple clime where the hills uprear
    Their stately towers of snow.

Oh! for the break of the silver sea
    On the bright Italian shore—
It were calm to the never-ceasing roll
    Of the dark Atlantic's roar!

I am sick of my life in this dreary isle,
    I am wearied to death of the rain;
Ah! when will the black clouds melt away,
    And the sun shine warm again!"

GWEN.

(For Music.)

Gwen, little Gwen, do I see you again?
Years have sped since we parted in pain,
Years of pleasure, methinks, to you
For I mark no change in your mien or hue,
Sweet and fair, as you were to me
In the golden summer of 'Eighty-three.

Gwen, little Gwen, when I met your glance
Suddenly now in the turn of the dance,
Back to my heart, with the surging blood,
The old thoughts swept in a tremulous flood,
But calm and cold was your look to me,
Not the look of my darling of 'Eighty-three!

Gwen, little Gwen, I am wondering now
When lovers in plenty before you bow,
When your soul is sated with flattery's sweets
And the pulse of pleasure too wildly beats,
Do you ever at all think kindly of me
And the golden summer of 'Eighty-three?

Gwen, little Gwen, if I not mistake,

There is one who would die for your sweet life's sake,

For look! in his eyes what a passionate gleam

As yon twain whirl round in the joyous stream!

Treat him kindlier, dear, than you treated me

In the golden summer of 'Eighty-three!

Gwen, little Gwen, we will say " Good-bye!"

Teacher and pupil were you and I :

You have forgotten, but I, poor fool,

Learnt my lesson too well in Love's gay school,

The lesson, you know, which you taught to me

In the golden summer of 'Eighty-three!

Gwen, little Gwen, 'tis our last " Farewell!"

Oh, that the heart could its yearnings tell!

Oh, that life had the joys of yore,

And the world the roses it whilom bore,

And you were still, as you were to me

In the golden summer of 'Eighty-three!

TO OUR GOOD BISHOP.

(On his recovery from severe illness).

Revered, respected by all ranks and years,
  The high, the low, the aged, and the young,
  With hearts rejoicing and exultant tongue,
We bid thee prosper, whose good life endears
The name of Bishop to the people! Tears
  Of grief were ours, had we been robbed of thee
  By Death's dark angel—joy instead shall be
On every face whence cloudy sadness clears
Since thou art spared!—Ah, pain indeed the thought,
"If we should lose him"—to each vexed heart
    brought!
Father-in-God, of Christ's words mindful aye,
"Feed thou My sheep—feed thou My lambs alway,"
In times like these where could we find us now
One wiser, kinder, more beloved than thou?

PART III.

Sacred Poems.

PART III.

SACRED POEMS.

ADVENT SUNDAY.
1889.

Through gloom and shade our lives are laid,
    Perplexity and sorrow,
With hearts that ache our way we take,
    Despairing of the morrow.

The stars grow pale, their cressets fail
    Along the ridge of heaven,
And Doubt's dark pall obscures for all
    What light the moon had given.

"Ah, for the day!" we sigh and pray,
  "The day of His returning,
To right the wrong that lasts too long,
  To calm the heart's deep yearning!"

O feeble minds, whom Satan blinds,
  So faint in faith's endeavour
Pray ye for grace to run the race,
  And win you Heaven for ever!

Far spent the night, the golden light
  Of dawn will soon be breaking.
Long, long and deep is earth's last sleep,
  But, oh, the glad awaking!

For Christ your King will come and bring
  His servants joy for sadness,
To each true heart His peace impart
  And everlasting gladness!

THE SOUTHERN CROSS.

The most conspicuous constellation in the heavens, in the southern hemisphere, and one never visible in our latitudes, is a brilliant group of four very bright stars, which form a cross in the sky, and thus are known by Astronomers as the Southern Cross. These few lines will explain the allusion in the following poem.

TO ONE BENEATH THE SOUTHERN CROSS.

The Cross shines clear in your midnight skies,
Telling wherein Redemption lies ;
As you watch it glowing on Noel Eve,
May your heart rejoice and in Christ believe.

Listen and you shall hear the song
Of the blissful angels borne along,
And tidings of Love that ne'er can cease
Shall fall upon you like perfect peace.

Oh, whatever the burden His wisdom sees
You should bear for Him, on your bended knees
Praising Him, blessing Him, thanking Him, say :
" Take not Thy cross from Thy servant away.

Be it on me and with me through all my life,
As I follow Thy steps in this mortal strife,
And uplift my soul at the last like Thee,
O'er death to triumph eternally ! "

IN THE TIME OF HARVEST.

Whose the heart bowed down with sadness
  On this high rejoicing day?
To His temple all in gladness
  Take with one consent their way,
     Praising, blessing,
     And confessing
God the King of kings for aye.

Autumn fields with plenty waving,
  Golden harvests crown the year!
Vain were mortal toil and slaving
  Had not God's good hand been near.
     Guarding, tending,
     And defending
From all danger, harm, and fear.

Larger bounties daily sending,
  For our wants He doth provide,
And His charity unending,
  Flows immeasurably wide.
     Praise Him, bless Him,
     And confess Him
Fount of heavenly pity's tide!

Oh, the mercies He has shown us,
 Oh, the gifts by grace bestowed,
"Sons of God" to call and own us,
 Washed and cleansed in Jesus' Blood!
  Praise Him, bless Him,
  And confess Him
God the giver of all good!

Yea, His care is constant o'er us,
 And His Hand is full and free,
And His Presence goes before us,
 And our strong Defence is He:
  Still He leads us,
  Guides us, feeds us,
Brings us safe where we would be!

Oh, that men would therefore praise Him
 For the works that He has done,
God, our Father, God, our Saviour,
 God, our Comfort, Three in One.
  Praise Him, bless Him,
  And confess Him,
Whilst eternal ages run! Amen.

IN THE HOSPITAL WARD.

The night is waning : draw aside, I pray you,
  The window curtains : let the grey dawn in !
No long time now shall I, kind nurse, delay you,
  My last long journey hence will soon begin !

Only a poor old waif and nothing better,
  I drifted lonely down the stream of life !
Fortune unkind—well, it were best forget her
  And go to sleep, oblivious of her strife !

When came I here?—was it not yester-even ?—
  You murmur something :—"Fourteen days ago!"
Strange !—I remember a cart madly driven—
  A crash—a fall !—and then, no more I know !

Ah, there were times I used to laugh and wonder
  What good a hospital could do to me ;
" A waste of money and a sort of blunder,"
  That's what I called it ! Now, its use I see,

And thankful am I that the Lord of pity
    Moved tender hearts to do a noble deed
Thus to have care for all who in this city
    In anguish lie, in sickness and in need.

Nurse dear—your face is very sweet and winning,
    Too good to hide beneath a cowl of black!—
Would you once more that story be beginning
    About the prodigal who wandered back?

"I will arise and go unto my Father"—
    Yes, I am going!—will He welcome now
With words of mercy His lost son? Or rather,
    Meet me with anger and unbending brow?

"His love's unfailing!"—Ah, but, nurse, I grieved Him
    Long, long ago when I was young and wild!
Once He was near to me, and I believed Him,
    Ay, and I loved Him when I was a child!

Pray for me will you? for your prayers, sweet maiden,
    Rise from pure lips and from a heart as pure:
Say that the old man's soul is heavy-laden,
    Say that he rest and pardon would secure!

" The Lord is very gracious and long-suffering ;
    He casts not out who come in tears to Him "—
But will He take so valueless an offering
    And this poor broken heart when life grows dim ?

Hold me one moment, hold me !—I am sinking
    In the deep waters—in this awful gloom !
It is not death from which my soul is shrinking,
    But—that beyond it—that eternal doom !

Nurse, nurse !—That light !—What shape of dazzling
    glory
    Comes from the East ?—He smiles—He smiles on
    me !
Pierced are His hands—His brow is marred and
    gory !—
    Jesus, my Saviour, let me cling to Thee !

VOICES OF EARTH AND HEAVEN.

"The world is dark and dreary ;
O brothers, we are weary !
   Where may we seek for rest ?
Sin everywhere prevailing,
Fierce doubt our faith assailing,
   What comforts the distressed ? "
Ah, never murmur, never falter !
   Bow meekly to the rod !
Leave all to One who cannot alter—
   Have faith in God !

"Friends fall away and grieve us,
Our dearest ones deceive us,
   And fail when most we trust :
Pride stern disaster humbles,
And Time each bright hope crumbles
   For ever into dust."
Ah, never murmur, never falter !
   Bow meekly to the rod !
Leave all to One who cannot alter—
   Have faith in God !

" Black skies are lowering o'er us,
The long, long night before us,
  We cannot see our way :
Oh, will the gloom and sorrow
Be merging, on the morrow,
  In everlasting day ? "
Ah, never murmur, never falter !
  Bow meekly to the rod !
Leave all to One who cannot alter—
  Have faith in God !

" Still forward—ever forward !
What sea is breaking shoreward ?
  We tremble at its roar !
By all in turn attempted—
No mortal yet exempted—
  Few reach the farther shore ! "
Ah, never murmur, never falter !
  Bow meekly to the rod !
Leave all to One who cannot alter—
  Have faith in God !

THE TRUE LIGHT.

Give light to me, O God!
    Light in my soul,
That I may clearly read
    The pages of that scroll
Thy hand unfolds in earth and sky and sea,
Discerning Thee in all, in all, adoring Thee.

Give light to me, O God!
    Light shed within,
That I may plainly see
    My heart in all its sin ;
And, conscience-stricken at its woeful case,
Loathe and condemn myself, and cry to Thee for grace.

Give light to me, O God!
    That, while I scan
Thy promises of peace
    And hope to fallen man ;
I to myself their precious balm may take,
And for my deadly wound a healing ointment make.

Give light to me, O God !
That, counting dross
All vain conceits of earth,
I may take up my cross ;
And climb those thorny steeps that lead above,
Following with patient feet the blood-marked steps
of Love.

Give light to me, O God !
That never doubt
May cloud my faith, or sin
The blissful view blot out ;
But clearer day by day before my eyes,
The far-off land appear, the pearly gates arise.

Give light to me, O God !
Through all my days.
Shine on me, lead me straight
In Thy most holy ways ;
Then, dim, impaired tho' bodily vision be,
I shall have light enough, True Light, beholding Thee.

EASTER HYMN.

(For Tune see Sullivan's first setting to No. 556 in "Church Hymns.")

O Morn of Light, serenely bright
On which thro' death's dark portal
Our glorious Sun, the triumph won,
    Came splendidly immortal!
    Exultant, we will welcome thee
    With songs of hope and gladness,
    For Christ, our need, is risen indeed
      And gives us joy for sadness.

Priest, Prophet, King!—What raptures spring
    In every heart recalling
How, by Thy pains, were burst the chains
    The soul of man enthralling!
Before Thee fell the powers of hell
    The grisly hosts of error:
Thy glorious sheen the world unseen
    Deprived of all its terror!

High let us raise our hymn of praise
   In thankful adoration
And tell the fame of Jesus' Name
   The giver of salvation!
For us He bled, endured, was dead,
   And in the grave lay lowly,
Subdued all foes, for us He rose
   The Lord of Life most holy!

O Morn of Light, serenely bright,
   Chased by thy beams undying
The winter-day of Earth away
   All panic-struck is flying!
Hail, gladdening Sun!—Thou hast undone
   The rule of Doubt for ever!
We know that Thou our God art now,
   Our Friend forsaking never! Amen.

.

A CLOUD WITH A SILVER LINING.

Years, like an idle dream,
   Pass soon away,
Nothing on earth remains
   Firm in one stay :
Jesu, true Light of light
Shine when death's gloomy night
   Falls on our day.

Shine on us in our weal,
   Solace our woe,
Point with Thy radiancy
   Where we should go ;
Rough though the way may be,
Yet that it leads to Thee
   Teach us to know.

Parting from friends we love,
　Seeing, with tears,
Snapt every tender link
　That life endears ;
Mourning an only child,
Angel of mercy mild,
　Calm Thou our fears.

Bring Heaven near to us,
　Open our eyes—
Take Thou the veil away
　Dark'ning the skies.
Grant that, like Stephen, we
Thee at God's right hand see
　Holding the prize !

Thou didst the Cross endure
　Help us to bear
That which in wisdom Thou
　Will'st us to share ;
Then, after painful fight,
Bid us, O Light of light,
　Rest with Thee *there !*

AS NIGHT CREEPS ON.

(Vox Stellarum. 10. 6. 10. 4.)

The Harmonies revised by Hamilton Robinson, Mus. Bac., F.C.O., Organist and Director of the Choir of St. Stephen's, South Kensington.

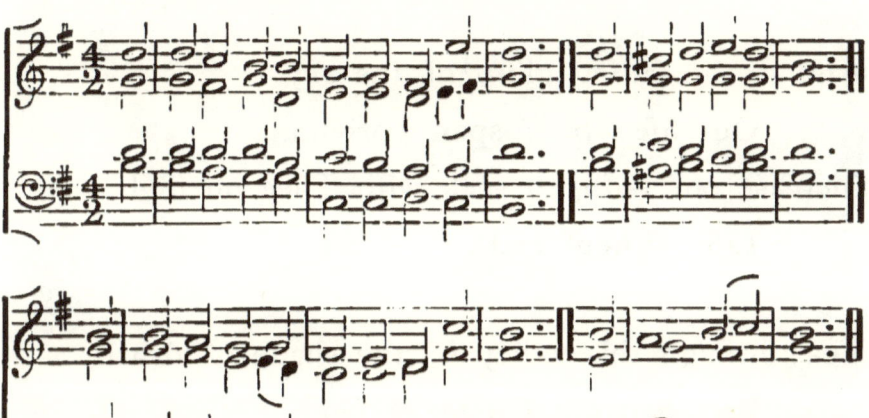

The day is dying, and around us fall
    Dark shadows of the night ;
Yet in our souls, Saviour and Friend of all,
    Let there be light !

Speak peace to minds that through past hours
    have been
    By worldly cares oppressed,
Assuage the sorrow, and forgive the sin
    Known to each breast.

Take from our eyes the sceptic mote and beam—
  Take from our hearts the doubt,
And let Thy face in clear unclouded gleam,
  Our Star, shine out !

And if the fading glory of the sky
  Our life's brief span portend,
Increase our faith, to seek with Thee on high
  Life without end.

Yea, through this valley of the shade of death,
  Be Thou our Guide, O God,
The stay and comfort of our parting breath
  Thy staff, Thy rod ! Amen.

"COME, LET US GO TO MARY'S SON"

In Nazareth of old, they say,
    Oft would the peasant folk repair
(Their hearts, along life's dreary way,
    Oppressed with anguish or despair)
To Joseph's lowly dwelling-place,
    To see the Saviour face to face.

"Come, let us go to Mary's Son!"—
    Anxious and careworn, was their cry—
"'Tis good to leave our tasks undone
    And, while He toils, stand watching by;
'Tis good His patient smile to meet
    And hear His words so calm and sweet!"

Dark care relaxed its sullen mien,
    Eyes dim with tears grew bright again,
And comfort and content were seen
    On hopeless brows dispelling pain,
For none drew near that gentle Friend
    But felt the better to the end.

And is He changed ?   And can He now
  No more console, no longer cheer,
Smooth out no wrinkles on the brow,
  Allay no grief and dry no tear ?
Not so : perennial springs above
  The well of Life, the fount of Love !

Still, whatsoever be the woe,
  The pain, the burden on our hearts,
'Tis good to Mary's Son to go,
  Who bliss bestows and hope imparts,
While tender hand and soothing voice
  Bid us look upward and rejoice.

O ye along life's dreary way
  Oppressed with anguish or despair,
Why will ye longer here delay
  Who should to Jesus Christ repair ?
Still in earth's lowliest, humblest place
  Seek ye Him out and watch His face !

In some poor cottage of the land,
  Or workshop, if ye are not blind,
Still shall ye see Him gently stand,

And hear His accents soft and kind ;
And learn, with new-born happiness,
Your souls in patience to possess.

Never far off, to mortal grief
Always He lends a ready ear,
Prompt to bestow the sure relief,
Quick to remove the weightiest fear,
And all may reach His sheltering side,
The path Repentance, Faith the guide.

Then straightway go to Mary's Son,
For He has much to give you all !
'Tis good to leave sin's tasks undone
And at His feet adoring fall ;
'Tis good from cark and care to cease,
To rest in God and be at peace !

U

"SEE HOW THESE CHRISTIANS HATE ONE ANOTHER!"

O pitiful display of self and spite!
   Headstrong delusion of a loveless age!
Is Christianity o'erwhelmed in night
   That Christians now, and not the heathen, rage?

Thousands are longing for the Bread of Life,
   And hands outstretched, in vain request, they hold,
While wrangle priests in internecine strife
   Whether the paten shall be clay or gold;

Whether the chalice that contains the wine
   Wherein true Faith finds such refreshing grace,
Shall be regarded as the more Divine,
   Uplifted, worshipped in the Saviour's place;

Whether the vestment shall be *this* or *that*,
   Or *here* or *there* the celebrant be seen,
Till plain folks wonder in amazement what
   The plain directions of the Prayer-Book mean!

"All for God's glory!" so men say, when lie
   Full oft forgotten on their dusty shelves
The gifts He gave them, and their words imply
   The mode they took to glorify themselves!

On our own feebleness we lean too much,
   Wishful by words to purge away all sin,
And less and less with Christ we are in touch
   To kindle, strengthen, deepen life within.

So, over rites and shibboleths and forms
   We waste our energies, and rant and rave,
While souls are lost in Passion's howling storms,
   And hopeless seek the dark, despairing grave.

Of old in Salem, when that awful hour
   Of utter desolation came, and gloom,
And on her battlements remorseless power
   The grasp had tightened of unaltering doom ;

Hemmed in on all sides, shot at, smitten, slain
   By sling and spear, by catapult and stone,
While gaunt Starvation, Fever's gnawing pain,
   Bade thousands perish, thousands weep and groan ;

How, then, behaved the wise men and the great,
　　The lords and rulers of that race ill-starred?
Ah, Factions raged, and fratricidal Hate,
　　A famished wolf with wolves contending, gnarred!

Jew butchered Jew until the streets ran red
　　With blood of victims whom the Roman steel
Had spared as captives! Love and Friendship dead,
　　It was as if the foe alone could feel!

So now, within our Salem's leaguered walls
　　Hemmed in by infidels, by doubts assailed,
Though here and there some staunch defender falls,
　　How few the few who have in faith prevailed!

No! All are wrangling, shrieking, battling still
　　Among themselves, in wrath and bitter spite,
For wretched whims and not the Master's will,
　　Contending ever in unholy fight!

Oh, shame upon us! If the end draws near—
　　"The end of all things"—churches, chapels, creeds,
Shall we His servants, in that final fear,
　　Best do Him service by our evil deeds?

Man? In the judgment, what will man avail?
　Who in the midst stand *then*, our plague to stay?
O Christ, our Priest, now passed within the veil,
　Thou, only Thou, our helper be that day.

Thou, only Thou, our God and Saviour *now*,
　Thou, only Thou, our God and Saviour *then*,
Bow to Thy will, O blessed Jesus, bow
　Th' unruly wills of miserable men!

"WHAT IS TRUTH?"

(A recollection of the late Canon Liddon.)

Saint Mary's Church at Oxford long ago ;
　The assizes on, the judges here attend ;
Thronged with the great is every bench below,
　And thronged the galleries from end to end.

I hear a sweet, low voice a text give out,
　The scoffer's question in the Judgment Hall,
And soon to Eloquence arraigning Doubt,
　In rapt attention men are listening all.

Ah, "What is Truth?"—not Pilate, judge unjust,
　With cynical insouciance asks alone :
Man to his Maker, to its God the dust,
　The same contempt for centuries has shown.

The careless world with mocking smile propounds
　The solemn question, scorning all reply—
Where falsehood rules and foolishness abounds,
　Christ and the Cross unheeded still go by !

And now the lips that pled His cause so well
　Are hushed for ever, and His servant true
(Who for his loss our bitter grief shall tell?)
　Rests and receives his recompense most due.

'Jesus is God, and over all shall reign,"
　Such was the message that he sought each day,
In weariness, in trials, and in pain,
　By lips and life unfaltering to convey.

And if ye ask, in lowly, docile wise,
　"What answer to the question put of old?"
Then would I say, "Ah, might ye not surmise
　That secret best by lives like Liddon's told?

To have proved ever loyal to the Right,
　Serene in age, as pure and brave in youth,
To have held fast by God in Doubt's dark night—
　This is the answer—*this* indeed is Truth!"

GOD'S WITNESSES.

(10. 6. 10. 4.)

W. P. Propert. Mus. Bac. Oxon.; LL.D. Cantab. Christmas, 1889.

Night after night in yon pellucid sky
    The solemn stars appear,
In proud array and marshalled pomp on high,
    Throughout the year.

The mighty armies of the Lord of Hosts,
    Along the azure plain
Their tents are pitched, and their unaltered posts
    Are duly ta'en.

The bright spears flash, the silvery falchions glow,
    Blood-red the banners gleam ;
To gaze upon them is indeed to know
    Earth's loveliest dream !

Night after night upon that ebon scroll,
    In characters of flame,
The great Archangels of the deep unroll
    Jehovah's Name.

While from the silence of that boundless space
    Comes to the soul a cry:
" Kneel, child of earth, and veil in awe thy face,
    Thy God is nigh ! "

THE ANGEL OF CONSOLATION.

Like a golden shaft of glory
  Down from the Throne I glide,
I enter the lowliest cottage,
  The stateliest halls of pride ;
Wherever a soul is bending
  'Neath sorrow's crushing pain,
I, the Angel of Consolation,
  Speak peace, and not in vain !

Wherever the Eye all-seeing
  Beholds in human frame
A heart that is laden with anguish
  And sad with sin and shame,
Forth on my errand of mercy
  Swifter than thought I speed,
With leaves from the Tree whose virtue
  Can salve all wounds that bleed.

Look ! From the gates of Eden,
  In misery and woe,
Man and his wife are driven
  Their doom to undergo,
Tears from their sad eyes streaming
  And in their hearts despair,
Though the flaming sword I brandished,
  Yet I whispered comfort there.

Alone in the howling desert
  Mother and son recline,
And oh, for a well of water
  How longingly they pine !
The voice of the lad is answered,
  By Hagar's side I stand,
And the cool, clear fount is bubbling
  Up from the arid sand !

And once, in the awful horror
  That fell on God's own Son
When the load was heaped upon Him
  Of sins which man had done,

When the face of the loving Father
   Turned stedfastly away—
Ah precious task !—through the darkness
   I came, a strengthening ray !

Look up, sad hearts, and break not !
   There is hope for all who toil !
Still the leaves of the Tree can heal you,
   Wells spring from the thirsty soil,
Still the Angel of Consolation,
   Who soothed the Christ's deep pain,
Comes to His humble servants,
   To strengthen, cheer, sustain.

S. PETER'S DAY, 1890.

"Feed My Lambs" and "Follow Me."

Night is waning, dawn is breaking,
　Jesus stands upon the shore,
Watching while His servants labour,
　Toiling, struggling evermore—
Ah, so little good effecting,
　And so much that they deplore !

Long and vain our best endeavours,
　Hands are feeble, worn are feet ;
Hark !—His voice across the waters
　Comes in accents clear and sweet,
Thrilling ev'ry heart that hears Him—
　" Children, have ye any meat ? "

" All the night, O Lord, we laboured,
　Nothing have we for our pains."
" Be not weary "—soft He answers—
　" Patient toil hath perfect gains—
Only he that loves and labours
　To the full reward attains ! "

Cast the net once more in faith, then,
   Trusting to the Master's care,
Present in our midst to bless us
   And to answer fervent prayer,
Ever to all hearts imparting
   Joy and gladness for despair !

Jesu, loving little children
   With an everlasting love,
Looking down in tender pity,
   Guarding them, from realms above,
Pour upon us of the fulness
   Of the gracious Heavenly Dove !

Thou to Thine Apostle, Peter,
   By the Galilean sea,
Strict command and thrice repeated,
   Test of truest love to be,
Gavest, in Thy risen glory,
   " Feed My Lambs," and " Follow Me."

Work in us, both priests and people,
   Strengthen us this charge to keep,
Mindful of our solemn duty,

Never at our posts asleep,
Lips and hearts the words repeating,
  "Feed My lambs" and "Feed My sheep!"

Help us, Lord, the young and feeble
  Well to guide along life's way,
Guarding, shepherding, defending
  From all paths that lead astray.
Till they reach the gates of Heaven,
  There to see Thy face for aye!

Help us, too, with more devotion
  In Thy steps to follow on,
Daily to that place ascending
  Whither Thou before art gone,
Bearing here our cross in patience
  Till the crown of life be won!

Praise to God our Heavenly Father,
  Praise to God our Saviour be,
Praise, Almighty Holy Spirit,
  Evermore be done to Thee,
To the ages of the ages
  God the Lord eternally! Amen.

THE MESSAGE OF THE BELLS.

Four hundred years the bells,
High in the belfry hung,
Through all the Seasons of the Church
Their solemn notes have rung.

On festival and fast,
The day when Christ was born,
On dark Good Friday's noon of woe,
On gladsome Easter morn,

With Holy Thursday's dawn,
At solemn Pentecost,
They bade the sinner think of Him
Who hath redeemed the lost.

Our fathers' fathers heard
The music which we hear,
" Oh, come and worship Christ the Lord
In lowly faith and fear ! "

And long before their day,
These iron tongues were raised,
And o'er the land the message pealed
"God's Holy Name be praised!"

And still the bells ring on,
As year by year goes by,
"O blessed Jesu, pray for us
And save us or we die!"

Each mournful funeral knell,
Each joyous Sunday chime,
Reminds us of our latter end,
The rapid flight of time!

What numbers lie asleep
Beneath yon grassy mounds,
Who once in life and strength despised
The warning of these sounds!

What numbers, too, who came,
Obedient to the call,
And found within our Father's House
That Christ is all-in-all!

x

O hear the solemn bells,
Good people, young and old !
Seek God and let His Name be praised
Ere your last hour be tolled !

Seek God in His own House—
Your fathers' God—and pray
That pardoning love and perfect peace
May rest on you for aye !

There, at the Holy Font
While faith's first rite is paid,
There, when the Sacred Feast is spread,
Kneel and implore His aid.

Seek Him with heart and soul
And His refreshing grace,
So in the light of Heaven at last
You shall behold His face !

THE UNINVITED GUEST.

"Thy faith hath saved thee : go in peace."

With drooping head and brow of shame,
   Timidly gliding through the street,
To Simon's house a woman came
   (The Nazarene sat there at meat) ;
Her eyes were red with weeping sore,
An alabaster box she bore.

At that proud board she sought no place,
   Unwelcome, uninvited guest ;
The pallor of her wistful face
   Hungered for nothing only rest,
And wine of earth had hateful grown
To lips athirst for God alone !

Sobbing she came and stood behind,
   And kissed the robe of Christ her Lord ;
In agony of thought and mind
   Down her worn cheeks the tear-drops poured,
Upon His blessed feet they fell,
The burden of her soul to tell.

With tears she washed them—tears of grief,
   For that past life of sin and wrong,
Then, when her woe had found relief,
   Low-kneeling, with her tresses long
She wiped them tenderly, and oft
Paused to imprint with kisses soft.

Then from her box the costly nard,
   These to anoint, she swiftly drew
While Simon in his heart so hard,
   Was murmuring : " If this man but knew
What manner of woman touched him so,
Resentment surely he would show ! "

But He, who read the thoughts of all,
   Knew why she came and what she did ;
He marked the tears of anguish fall,
   Nor was the heart's repentance hid ;
Disdained not He the sinner's touch
Who, much forgiven, lovèd much !

So from His lips the words proceed
   That fill her broken heart with joy,
And satisfy her utmost need

And dark despair with light destroy :
His pardon gave her soul release—
" Thy faith hath saved thee, go in peace ! "

O Christ our Lord, enthroned on high,
   Thou knowest all our wants and needs,
And Thou with penetrating eye
   Canst search the heart that inly bleeds,
O hear us, save us, help us now
Who penitent before Thee bow !

To-day, as in the days of old,
   All power in heaven and earth is Thine !
Years cannot make Thy love grow cold,
   Friend of the fallen, Life Divine !
Speak but the word—our sins forgive,
And we " in peace " henceforth shall live !